Immortal C
Annive

N.

Mandy M. Roth, Online

Mandy loves hearing from readers and can be found interacting on social media.

(copy & paste links into your browser window)

Website: http://www.MandyRoth.com

Blog: http://www.MandyRoth.com/blog

Facebook: http://www.facebook.com/AuthorMandyRoth

Twitter: @MandyMRoth

Book Release Newsletter: mandyroth.com/newsletter.htm

(Newsletters: I do not share emails and only send newsletters when there is a new release/contest/or sales)

Immortal Ops

Paranormal Shifter Military Special Ops Romance

Immortal Ops Team Captain Lukian Vlakhusha is having issues with his newest target, Peren Matthews. His higher-ups want her eliminated. He simply wants her. The alpha side of him demands he claim her — that is, if she'll have him. After all, he's what she fears most — a wolf shifter. But there is more to Peren than even she's aware of and the enemy is closer than anyone imagined.

Suggested Reading Order of Books Released to Date in the Immortal Ops Series World

This list is NOT up to date. Please check MandyRoth.com for the most current release list.

Immortal Ops

Critical Intelligence

Radar Deception

Strategic Vulnerability

Tactical Magik

Act of Mercy

Administrative Control

Act of Surrender

Broken Communication

Separation Zone

Act of Submission

Damage Report

Act of Command

Wolf's Surrender

The Dragon Shifter's Duty

And more (see Mandy's website & sign up for her newsletter for notification of releases)

Books In Each Series Within The Immortal Ops World.

This list is NOT up to date. To see an updated list of

the books within each series under the umbrella of the Immortal Ops World please visit MandyRoth.com. Mandy is always releasing new books within the series world. Sign up for her newsletter at MandyRoth.com to never miss a new release.

You can read each individual series within the world, in whatever order you want...

PSI-Ops
Act of Mercy

Act of Surrender

Act of Submission

Act of Command

Act of Command

And more (see Mandy's website & sign up for her newsletter for notification of releases)

Immortal Ops
Immortal Ops

Critical Intelligence

Radar Deception

Strategic Vulnerability

Tactical Magik

Administrative Control

Separation Zone

And more (see Mandy's website & sign up for her newsletter for notification of releases)

Immortal Outcasts

Broken Communication

Damage Report

And more (see Mandy's website & sign up for her
newsletter for notification of releases)

Shadow Agents

Wolf's Surrender

The Dragon Shifter's Duty

And more (see Mandy's website & sign up for her
newsletter for notification of releases)

**Crimson Ops Series and Paranormal Regulators
Series (Part of the Immortal Ops World) Coming Soon!**

Dedication and Note from the Author

To the fans of the Immortal Ops Series, thank you for your continued dedication and for your love of the I-Ops. I can't believe it's been *well* over a decade since Immortal Ops book one was first published (2004) and even longer since it was first written. I will forever be thankful to my father for instilling in me a love of science fiction; to my grandfather for giving me such a love of history that I found myself fascinated with what the world would have been like if events ended differently — or maybe didn't end at all (hint, hint); to my mother who has always told me to dream big; to my brother who was the first victim (big grin) of listening to me tell tales; to my husband for telling me to keep going, not to give up even when it seemed like the best choice; to my sons who have brought me so much happiness (and a new appreciation for stain removal tips and tricks, not to mention making me quite the skilled cut and scrape fixer); and last but not least, to everyone who has fallen in love with my characters and encouraged me to keep writing. I can't thank you all enough for your support. In addition, I'd like everyone to remember the men and women in the Armed Services who are, at this very moment, putting their lives on the line for our freedom.

A note from the author about the expanded editions and what inspired The Immortal Ops:

Many things combined to create the perfect storm, if you will, for how I came up with the series idea well over a decade ago. Having been heavy into marketing and advertising and then suddenly finding myself needing to stay home to care for my boys, one of whom had additional needs, I was left craving a creative outlet.

I first tried to get my "fix" by playing video games after the boys were asleep at night. I was online and playing the first day Xbox Live launched (November 2002). I found myself getting very into first-person-shooters and military games. The more I got into playing video games, the more I wanted to read about the actual history behind the games. I found myself talking with friends who had served our country. I would devour anything they wanted to offer, listening, completely swept up in it all. Each story shared a common theme — a strong sense of brotherhood.

This appealed to me, and in a relatively short period of time, I decided to do something about it. That impulse, combined with my love of history, science fiction, the paranormal, and technology, as well as my love of things that go bump in the night, really was a recipe for the Immortal Ops Series to be born from my imagination. From a very early age, I've been fascinated with the supernatural, myths and legends. I have always read books that revolve around the supernatural. I cut my teeth on Stephen King, Clive Barker, Anne Rice, and the classics. Two books that made a huge impression on me were *The Island of Dr. Moreau,* and of course *Dracula*.

The more I found myself digging into the history of the military and of world wars, the more I kept getting this thought in the back of my brain, pushing me forward. Urging me to combine both loves — supernatural and history. I thought, what would happen if I took a team of men who were in the military, and they were a paramilitary group, a black ops type of thing, and I combined them with my love of the paranormal?

The scary part about the Ops series is that it was born from events that actually happened in history, just with a large fictional spin put on it. I asked myself, what if I took from history, from eugenics, which so many assume started in Nazi Germany, and threaded it into the very fabric of the military team? What if I were to take a page from history and the horrible cross-breeding attempts made by Ilya Ivanov and the Nazis to create super-soldiers, who were ape and human hybrids? And what if I were to weave in even more aspects, like cloning, additional genetic engineering, and so on? What if I went a step beyond and brought in other parts of history that revolve around attempts at making super-soldiers or controlling the minds of humans?

What would happen?

What would you be left with? How damaged would the men be? What kind of government would do this? What if I were to build off the history of it all, have it where America made super-soldiers behind the scenes, and then drew back and wanted to cut ties and stop everything when Nazi Germany rose and the backlash from that hit, but, in reality, they didn't stop? And with scientific advances, how would that work? What would it look like? The answer seemed simple to me. Take all these questions to what I felt was their logical conclusion and to also blend in what I love — werecreatures and vampires.

So the idea to have shape-shifting military men who were created by the government was born. And that was how I came up with The Immortal Ops Series. I started writing in 2000: thoughts, ideas, very short stories, and then full novels and novellas. The Ops were among the first things I put together and it wasn't long after that I was published (early 2004). My then-editor asked me if I could write something that was third-person point of view, instead of first-person, which I had first been published in. Since I had the Ops already started and the series all mapped out, it was just a matter of getting it to work as a third-person book, rather than first. Honestly, I wasn't sure I could. I'd mapped the series originally to be first-person. It took some elbow grease, but in the end it worked and the first four books were published. Reader support for them has been amazing.

Sadly, I found I had to cut a lot to make the book fit with word count restrictions then, but I'm happy to report that I have the rights back, and the first four books are being re-released with their original content.

Thank you,
Mandy M. Roth

Praise for Mandy M. Roth's Immortal Ops World

Silver Star Award—*I feel Immortal Ops deserves a Silver Star Award as this book was so flawlessly written with elements of intrigue, suspense and some scorching hot scenes*—Aggie Tsirikas—Just Erotic Romance Reviews

5 Stars—*Immortal Ops is a fascinating short story. The characters just seem to jump out at you. Ms. Roth wrote the main and secondary characters with such depth of emotions and heartfelt compassion I found myself really caring for them*—Susan Holly —Just Erotic Romance Reviews

Immortal Ops packs the action of a Hollywood thriller with the smoldering heat that readers can expect from Ms. Roth. Put it on your hot list...and keep it there! —The Road to Romance

5 Stars—*Her characters are so realistic, I find myself wondering about the fine line between fact and fiction...This was one captivating tale that I*

did not want to end. Just the right touch of humor endeared these characters to me even more — eCataRomance Reviews

5 Steamy Cups of Coffee — *Combining the world of secret government operations with mythical creatures as if they were an everyday thing, she (Ms. Roth) then has the audacity to make you actually believe it and wonder if there could be some truth to it. I know I did. Nora Roberts once told me that there are some people who are good writers and some who are good storytellers, but the best is a combination of both and I believe Ms. Roth is just that. Mandy Roth never fails to surpass herself —* coffeetimeromance

Mandy Roth kicks ass in this story — inthelibraryreview

Immortal Ops Series Helper

Immortal Ops (I-Ops) Team Members

Lukian Vlakhusha: Alpha-Dog-One. Team captain, werewolf, King of the Lycans. Book: Immortal Ops (Immortal Ops)

Geoffroi (Roi) Majors: Alpha-Dog-Two. Second-in-command, werewolf, blood-bound brother to Lukian. Book: Critical Intelligence (Immortal Ops)

Doctor Thaddeus Green: Bravo-Dog-One. Scientist, tech guru, werepanther. Book: Radar Deception (Immortal Ops)

Jonathon (Jon) Reynell: Bravo-Dog-Two. Sniper, weretiger. Book: Separation Zone (Immortal Ops)

Wilson Rousseau: Bravo-Dog-Three. Resident smart-ass, wererat. Book: Strategic Vulnerability (Immortal Ops)

Eadan Daly: Alpha-Dog-Three. PSI-Op and handler on loan to the I-Ops to round out the team, Fae. Book: Tactical Magik (Immortal Ops)

Colonel Asher Brooks: Chief of Operations and point person for the Immortal Ops Team. Book: Administrative Control (Immortal Ops)

Chapter One

Captain Lukian Vlakhusha walked through the halls of Immortal Ops headquarters, slightly disappointed to be back to work since he'd only had one week away at his estate in Maine. It had been a much-needed break. He owned nearly three hundred acres of wooded land that served well to keep who and what he was far from the prying eyes of humans. To keep him far from anyone being able to see what went on when he was home — how the woods seemed to burst at the seams with wolves whenever he was there. Or how the howls of packs of wolves could be heard for miles as his followers gave in to the moon's pull and the need to run and feel the wind on their faces. And most importantly, no humans were close to see those same wolves shape-shift into human form when they were done running free.

That was a biggie.

He loved his primary home but didn't get to spend nearly enough time there. Not with his current obligations and duties. Ones he'd taken on out of a sense of honor, not for need of the paycheck. He came from old money and didn't require any more. The estate had been in his family for generations, and he saw to its upkeep but felt no need to expand upon it. The main home on the property was big enough as it was. He'd picked up a two-engine plane several years ago to make the distance between his main home and work headquarters a much shorter travel. He didn't love to fly so much as he liked knowing he was the one in command of his fate, not some commercial pilot who may or may not have tied a few over before a scheduled flight.

Lukian tried to get home as much as possible, but work kept him busy. He had hired help back at the estate as well as trusted friends who came and went often, helping to oversee things there. His main concern was always his horses. The ironic part of it was, horses were notorious for being temperamental around supernaturals. He chuckled, remembering more than once in his immortally long life when a horse had decided it wanted nothing to do with him. Once while he was riding one. That ended with Lukian being unceremoniously dumped onto his backside.

Even with their unpredictability around supernaturals, he kept horses at his estate because he'd always been drawn to them, and while it had taken a while for them to trust him, they'd found a rhythm that worked well for them. They understood he didn't see them as lunch, and he understood they weren't at the point they'd let him ride them. At least not yet.

He chuckled as he thought of the horse he'd ironically named Gentle. It had bitten him several times already and had one hell of a temper. He couldn't blame the horse. It had been a rescue from an animal hoarder who had barely fed it and kept it locked up. Now, Gentle had wide-open fields and food. And a temper.

Lukian grinned. The horse had earned its foul mood.

He drew in a long breath, missing being home more and more as of late. He had a place not far from headquarters, but it didn't feel like home. It was simply somewhere he used to lay his head. It wasn't what Maine offered him—the privacy and all the acreage where he could let his inner beast out to run free. As a natural-born wolf shifter, or lycan as he preferred, he had to be sure to care for his beast side or run the risk of it overpowering him. He'd seen it happen to countless alpha males who thought they had a handle on their animal side, and it wasn't pretty.

He'd even had to hunt and put a number of those males down in his lifetime.

His chest tightened at the thought of it. He hated that side of the job. Hated having to kill his own kind.

Don't go there mentally, he thought. If he dared to let himself enter that dark headspace, he'd not recover. And in the end it would be others hunting him. Others stopping him from doing harm.

For now, he needed to remain calm and be thankful for the limited downtime he'd been granted. The lull before the storm. He and his men had worked long hours and months before they'd been given some leave. The break had been much needed, but not nearly long enough. He could have used another few weeks. It would take him at least that long to get Gentle to quit trying to take a chunk out of him.

He laughed softly.

It might take longer.

An announcement played overhead through the sound system, letting the men know of an update in the Middle East. The state of affairs from all over the world were monitored at the facility and every detail was shared with them, as if they alone could right all the wrongs.

The report had barely finished before another started. I-Ops HQ didn't provide much in the way of peace and quiet.

He sighed, missing the silence the time away had provided. The entire week away had been relaxing. No demands from those who were under him.

No weapons.

No violence.

Nothing but peace and solitude.

His primal instincts to hunt and kill were somehow sated when he was able to shift forms and run free. It was one of only a few activities that seemed to keep the beast at bay. Sex was another, but it often came with strings of attachment. Women always wanted more than he could give. They wanted a future with him. That wasn't an option. He wasn't a fish to be caught.

Nope. I'm a free agent and damn happy to be one, he thought with a grin.

He'd seen pack members meet their mates, and it left them testosterone-driven nutcases. That just wasn't for him. He didn't have time to grovel after some dame in a skirt. He had missions to worry about.

Not pussy.

That came easy enough.

Working helped to a degree as well. It kept him busy. He loved his job, he really did, but there were times it ate at his soul. What he and his team saw on a daily basis could give a normal man nightmares. Lukian was hardly normal. He also wasn't human. When he was young, he'd longed to be like the mortals. He'd wanted to blend with them, instead of hiding who and what he truly was—a creature humans thought existed only in fiction and fables. With age came wisdom and acceptance of things he could not change.

Though he found himself still envying humans to some degree. They lived in total ignorance to what went on around them in the world. They bought into whatever lie their governments or religious leaders spoon-fed them, and they seemed relieved to have stories of weather balloons in place of aliens. Hell, they had a show dedicated to the search for Bigfoot, yet all around them supernatural wonders existed. There was a naiveté about them that was appealing to an extent. It did border on stupid, so there was the issue of the fine line.

He shrugged. No use thinking about it anymore, as it could not be changed and he was what he was—part man, part beast. A lycan or man who could shift into a wolf and who had been born that way, not infected with the virus that created werewolves or other werecreatures. Lukian wasn't just any old lycan either. No. Lukian's bloodline was royal, leaving him in charge of the wolves in North America.

If only he'd taken to the political side of it all. He held the title of king but did little in the way of day-to-day needs the position required. He left that up to his advisers, who convened monthly at his home in Maine and then returned to their homes across the states, on call when need be. Lukian bucked the system and tradition. He chose instead to work— something his uncles still couldn't wrap their minds around. All of his uncles were on his advisory panel, and most were tolerant of his new ways, but one wasn't. One seemed to make it his mission to stand in opposition to everything Lukian tried to do as far as ruling.

Dick, he thought as he continued down the hall.

He rubbed his palms against his cloth-covered thigh, his body ready for a good run in the woods. The wolf side of him longed for the freedom to do as it pleased. What it was born to do. Wisely, the grounds of Headquarters were kept stocked with wild game. It was better he and his men hunt for animals rather than humans. That never went over well and always left more paperwork than anyone wanted to bother with.

Chapter Two

Lukian paused as one of his teammates approached. Geoffroi "Roi" Majors sang a song from a children's television show as he walked down the hall of Immortal Ops Headquarters past Lukian. Roi's ink-black hair hung to his shoulders and looked as if he'd just come from a shower. Lukian momentarily wondered what woman his friend had probably spent the night with. It wasn't often Roi slept alone. Lukian liked women just as much as the next guy, but Roi lived for them.

"Howdy, Captain. I'd ask if you'd be my neighbor, but I couldn't stand to hear you turn me down," said Roi with a tiny salute. He touched his chest. "It would break my heart. The wolf in me would curl up and die, and I'm sure I couldn't go on. Want to hold me close and tell me your love for me will never die? Come on, give Roi some sugar." He reached out, trying to hug Lukian, his lips puckered.

"I will shoot you if you kiss me," Lukian replied, though he was used to Roi's odd song choices and bizarre behavior. Honestly, Lukian was happy Roi had finally stopped whistling the theme song to a show that centered on the sheriff of a town called Mayberry. It had been getting so bad that Lukian had actually considered tearing the man's tongue out just to get him to shut up. As an alpha werewolf, he found it hard to resist the urge, but somehow, he managed.

It was difficult.

"Late start?" he asked, nodding his head to Roi's wet hair. While I-Ops Headquarters was state of the art, and it did have nice showers and locker rooms, the men preferred the comforts of their own homes. Roi's showering on location meant he'd not been home yet. That wasn't much of a surprise. Roi's playboy ways were getting out of control. Already the men had had to intervene and pick him up more than once when an angry female had tossed him out of her house while he was wearing nothing more than what he was born in and too drunk to shift forms and make it anywhere but to a ditch by the side of the road.

Lukian was hardly a monk, but his friend was taking womanizing to the extreme. One of these days he'd mess with the wrong woman, and she'd capture his heart and his dick. That would teach him. Lukian couldn't wait to see that happen.

"Guess what I spent my night doing?" Roi waggled his brows, a shit-assed grin spreading over his face. "Twins."

Lukian smiled despite himself. As much as he wanted to chastise the guy, a part of him found it amusing. He'd been young once, though he didn't look much older than his early thirties, and he had probably chased as much tail as Roi, maybe more. Now that he was older he knew that no matter how many women he fucked, he'd never truly be satisfied. None had been his mate. Until he found her, the one woman who would make his immortal soul whole, he'd always have an empty spot inside. The same void Lukian tried to pretend didn't exist. "You never stop, do you?"

"You know, you're king, you should really get twin action too." Roi tousled his wet hair, sending drops of water flying in all directions. "Chicks dig you."

Lukian disliked his title—by birthright—being brought up in conversation. He wasn't king of *all* the lycans. Just the American ones. He didn't wear his kinghood on his sleeve as did some royals he knew. France's king of Lycans was a total douchebag. The guy was a whiny little bitch who pranced around shouting his title for all to hear. As if anyone gave a shit. The last time the heads of the lycan councils gathered for a meeting, Lukian gave up trying to stop Roi from killing the guy, and hoped Roi would be successful.

Grinning, Roi lifted his arms out. "Seriously, you should live it up a bit, you're king."

Lukian considered shooting his longtime friend and right-hand man just to shut the guy up. Seemed like a waste of a bullet though since Roi wouldn't learn any lesson from it and he'd just heal the wound over within an hour. He gave Roi a disapproving look.

Roi shrugged. "I'd bang triplets if I was

king."

"You already bed triplets," answered Lukian, his voice even. Roi's position in the pack, which was second only to Lukian, held no bearing on how many women Roi bedded. The man could be pack beta and he'd still have a new woman next to him nightly.

Playboy Roi.

The nickname seemed to suit him.

Roi laughed. "Right. I do. What's four of 'em called? Is there a saying for that?"

"Yes. Man-whore."

Dr. Green entered from the other end of the hall. The man looked intimidating, tall, auburn hair, green eyes, and packed with muscle, but Lukian knew the truth—Green was a gentle giant. Books and all things science applied to Green. The shifter side of things—killing and death—did not. Though, Lukian suspected that if push ever came to shove, Green would not be a man he wanted to cross.

Green groaned as he looked in Roi's direction. "How many women this time?"

Roi held up two fingers and smiled wider.

Green glanced at Lukian. "One of these days he's going to regret having sex with every woman he meets."

"Probably not today though," Lukian said, moving closer to Green. The man picked science and the never-ending quest for knowledge over a social life. He hadn't always been that way. Once, long ago, Green had given the majority of his time to the woman he loved. Her death changed him. "What did you do with your downtime?"

"Read over some medical journals and attended three different seminars. One was especially good. It was about biometric engineering. They're doing some innovative things in the area, and I believe they could benefit wounded soldiers. And another seminar I attended was about signature-tagging mutagenesis. That was interesting as well."

Lukian held up a hand to stop Green. He'd go on and on if he didn't. The man's love of all things nerdy knew no limits. Lukian didn't have time to listen to a long, drawn-out discussion at the moment.

Roi's eyes widened with alarm. "You spent your downtime learning?"

Lukian nearly laughed at the horrified look on Roi's face. Roi wouldn't be caught dead in any sort of seminar unless it was on the finer points of picking up women. He'd be the one hosting the thing.

"I did," Green responded. "Very enlightening. There is another seminar not far from here in about three weeks. You're both welcome to attend with me."

Lukian froze. He did not want to attend any seminar with Green.

"Captain," Roi said, putting his hand on Green's shoulder as they both faced Lukian. "We really need to get this man laid, stat. I think we should make this priority number one."

While Roi had a point, Lukian knew better than to suggest such a thing to Green. The man had his own personal demons that kept him out of anyone's bed, and Lukian didn't question it. There was no point.

Plus, it wasn't as if Lukian had that many women warming his bed at nights as of late. He and Green must have looked like monks compared to Roi and his ways with the ladies.

To each his own.

They made their way into the conference room as Green continued to mumble something about alternating gene-expression patterns. Lukian glanced at Roi, already knowing Roi wasn't following the line of conversation. Lukian wasn't either. "I have no idea what he's talking about."

Roi shrugged. "I only understand about five percent of what he says when he starts talking about science crap."

"Five percent? Really?" Lukian doubted very much the percentage was even that high.

"It is really basic," said Green, lifting a hand as if he were about to launch into a lecture.

Lukian grabbed the man's hand and released it quickly. "Green, we're good. You'd be wasting your breath on us. We're lost causes with this stuff."

"Okay then," replied Green.

The men found their other team members already seated in the conference room. Field operative Lance Toov gave a small wave, and if Lukian didn't know better, he'd have sworn Lance tucked a dart gun below the table. Lance was a werepanther and dedicated team member, but he was also a practical jokester. It would be very like Lance to try to sneak a toy into a briefing.

Jon Reynell, a weretiger and the team's sniper, looked far away in thought, but Lukian knew the man heard everything that went on around him. Jon had always been the quietest of the team members and seemed to often get lost in self-reflection. That was probably what made him such a great sniper — he had patience where the rest of the team suffered from a distinct lack of it.

Wilson Rousseau, team smart-ass and wererat, was leaning back in his chair, fast asleep, his feet on the conference table. He was a fantastic operative, well-rounded and able to fill in wherever he was needed, but he didn't take much seriously. That was both good and bad.

Colonel Asher Brooks stood at the center of the room, near a whiteboard. Of all the men, the colonel was certainly the most clean-cut. At various points in Lukian's life he'd been the same way, but it never lasted long. He liked the slightly unkempt version of himself best. It was also the easiest to maintain.

Brooks never seemed fazed by much. Lukian had never been sure what Brooks was, but he knew enough to know the man wasn't human. The guy hadn't aged once in the years he'd known him, and he had no scent. None whatsoever. That wasn't normal. Not by a long shot. The only people he knew who could mask their scent were supernaturals, and none of them could do it to the degree the colonel could. All Lukian knew for sure was the guys who ran the show would never leave a human in charge of trying to corral the I-Ops. That would be unwise.

Very unwise.

On his way to his seat, Lukian kicked

Wilson's chair out from under him, sending the man crashing to the floor, jolting him awake. Wilson came up fast, his hair going in all directions, his claws erect, looking wild-eyed and as if he were ready to take on the world. "Who's your daddy?"

All men present simply stared at Wilson. Lukian blinked several times, trying to make sense of the question. Wilson knew who Lukian's father was. All the Ops did. "What kind of question is that?"

Roi leaned and lowered his voice, not that it mattered since the I-Ops had super sensitive hearing. "Slang thing. You wouldn't get it, old-timer."

Growling, Lukian showed fang in a playful manner. He enjoyed the light banter between the men and knew it was good for morale. They sometimes entered into some dark shit, and the ability to laugh and make light of things was needed. It was often all that kept a man sane. And he'd know, he'd seen enough of their brethren crack under the pressures of the Ops program. Seen their minds and spirits break. He wouldn't lose any more.

He'd lost too many already.

The history of the Ops program was steeped in horror and atrocities. Unspeakable ones. When science and politics mingled, the results often were less than pleasant. Years ago, Lukian had started to hear rumors of what the government was doing, but he'd dismissed them as fables. When he'd learned the truth, he'd been horrified and outraged. That got him nowhere. In the end he was simply one man, and he couldn't ask his followers to wage a war against factions of the government that were acting without the knowledge of the rest. He couldn't risk it getting even more out of control and humans finding out supernaturals were real.

That would end in a bloodbath.

So he'd gone to the source, to the places rumored to be conducting experiments on men and women. What he had found still sickened him to this day. History told the tale of mad scientists like Ilya Ivanov and his ape-army project—when he had tried to cross-breed apes and humans to make super-soldiers. History also spoke of Nazi's Eugenics and master races, but it did not tell the tale of the Immortal Ops program or any of the other tests that were done on a global level to try to make men better — to make them all they could be and more. No, history failed to mention any of that, but Lukian had seen it with his own eyes and he'd stepped in to try to make a difference. He'd offered his pure lycan blood, and that of other full-blooded shifters and supernaturals, as samples to use in place of whatever it was the scientists had cooked up. He'd done so against his advisers' wishes, and men had lived because of his actions. Good men. Like those in the room with him.

Men he thought of as family.

Roi snickered, pulling Lukian from his thoughts. It was for the best. Lukian didn't want to go down that dark path again.

His second-in-command pointed at Wilson and then spoke, "Sit down. No one is scared of a rat."

"Bite me, asshole," mouthed Wilson as he

sat and adjusted his T-shirt as if it were out of place. He flipped Roi off with both hands and then ran his hands through his hair, trying to look as if he wasn't acting like a teenager.

"Can I eat him?" asked Roi, a child-like quality suddenly in his voice.

Brooks set a file on the table, pulling attention to himself. "No." The screen behind Brooks lit up. "Gentlemen, I trust you had some good downtime."

"I did," said Roi, still grinning about his double action. "Green didn't. He learned all through his break. That is just sick and wrong. There are women to see and do."

Brooks paid Roi little mind. "Now, first order of business. We have an elimination order that has come in."

The men stiffened. Elimination orders were always touchy subjects. There had been more and more as of late, leaving the men feeling more like a hit squad than trained super-soldiers.

"Who?" asked Lukian.

"Tell me it's a vampire," said Roi with a

smile. "I hate vampires."

"Me too," added Jon, suddenly seeming to be involved in what was happening around him.

"Me three," said Wilson, right before an orange dart appeared on his forehead, sticking there.

Lance burst into hysterical laughter.

Lukian gave him a stern look. "Children."

With a shrug, Lance handed over the dart gun. "I've been waiting for thirty minutes to do that."

Wilson pulled the dart from his forehead. "Asshole."

Brooks groaned. "Are we done?"

"Yes, Colonel," the men said, glancing nervously at Lukian.

Lukian motioned to Brooks. "Continue."

Brooks shook his head. "Sorry, boys, no vamps. The target is a woman."

The men gasped. They had never been sent to eliminate a woman before. Lukian cast Brooks a questioning look, and Brooks sighed, seeming as displeased with the idea of it as

Lukian was. Brooks pushed the file toward Lukian, and Lukian opened it, his gaze whipping at once to the picture.

It took all of him not to stand and shout *mine*. Unsure where the urge was coming from and why he was having it, Lukian clasped his hands together and sat back in his seat quickly, as if the picture was some sort of juju set forth to bring out crazed proclamations from him.

Mine.

"Gentlemen," said Brooks. "This is Peren Matthews and she's the target. This came in as a high priority, but the details are sketchy at best. All I know is, the higher-ups want her eliminated. You have your orders. Make it happen."

Chapter Three

Peren sat and listened to her friends go on and on about their stressful week. They'd been trying to outdo one another for the greater part of an hour, possibly more, but she'd been successful in blocking them out to some degree. They were going on this outing for her benefit but she couldn't seem to muster the energy and will to be happy. She'd been doing her best to avoid social interactions for months now.

And her best friends had had enough of her behavior.

She turned her attention to the window and stared out at the night sky. Her gaze flickered to the crescent-shaped moon, and she had to fight the urge to trace the edges of it with her fingers. She'd always been obsessed with the wonders of night. As a small child she'd sit in her window and long to be among the stars. They seemed so peaceful, so free from care or concern. That had been what she wanted most as a child — peace. Now, on her twenty-fourth birthday, she sat in the back of Melanie's cramped Ford sedan and tried to wish herself somewhere serene. She found little amusement in the fact that she'd come full circle.

She shifted awkwardly in the seat and pushed the pile of used tissues away from her feet. Melanie was far from a neat freak, and the lipstick-stained tissues on the floor told her that Mel had a habit of tossing trash behind her as she drove.

Missy fixed her dark brown eyes on Peren and looked dismayed. "Girl, you need to lighten up—it's your birthday."

Peren let a fake smile creep onto her face. *Yeah, because it's so easy to lighten up knowing Kyle's gone and he'll never be back. It's wrong to be celebrating with him not here.* She tried to hide the emotions on her face, but Missy's expression told her she'd failed.

She couldn't get angry with Missy or Melanie. They were only trying to help. Since Kyle's disappearance, they'd gone out of their way to try to help her deal with her loss and move on. "You need to climb back up on that dick again, darling…that's bound to make you feel better." Mel had told her this on more than one occasion. Sure, she still had the same desires as the next woman, maybe even more, but moving on was the last thing on her mind. She just wanted to go home, curl up, listen to sad music, and wallow. She didn't need or want their planned interventions.

"Let's go to that new country music club… you know…" Melanie said, eyeing Missy in a way that said they'd already picked the destination long before the conversation started, "the one that has the line dancing. Maybe we could find some hot guys there tonight."

Peren sighed. She was committed to them for the rest of the night — their prisoner until dawn. She'd agreed to be a willing captive, and they'd agreed to leave her alone about dating other men. Most of their blind-date choices had been disasters. The first two were your typical college guys. They had one thing on their mind, and that was to get into her pants.

Melanie was upset that Peren hadn't given in to their advances. Sure, they were hot and she could have used a good fuck, but she wanted something more.

The third guy they'd fixed her up with, Ben, had been decent enough. His short black hair and light blue eyes had made for a fantastic combination. His conversational skills were far better than any of the men she'd been out with before. That wasn't the best thing about him, though. The best thing had been his smell. As silly as it sounded, he smelled like musk and fresh morning air. Kyle had had that very same natural scent. It drove her wild with lust.

Missy had been most surprised to find out that she'd gone on multiple dates with Ben. She'd really enjoyed his company, but felt guilty about betraying Kyle and cut it off. The nameless, faceless other dates meant so little to her that she'd lost count of them.

Missy faced forward. "I think Peren is totally ignoring us now."

Melanie sighed loudly. "I think you're

right. After a few drinks she'll be better."

"Isn't everyone?" questioned Missy, bringing the slightest of smiles to Peren's lips.

Chapter Four

"Do you smell that?" Lukian asked of Roi, who only just managed to stop trying to leave their place of concealment in search of new hotties to bang for the night. Mission be damned if women were involved. At least according to Roi's outlook on life as of late. He liked to look at it as saving a woman from going unsatisfied. Lukian saw it more as ignoring his duties.

"Smells like teen spirit all right," Roi said, his tongue running across his lips. He looked a little too eager for Lukian's liking.

Lukian ignored the comment because he'd known Roi long enough to know what his tastes in women were, and teenage girls weren't one of them.

His focus drew to a group of young women entering the nightclub they'd been camped out in front of for two hours, watching from an area where they wouldn't be spotted. Nope, not the ones they were in search of. These girls didn't look legal, which had prompted Roi's comment about teen and spirit.

"Tell me again why we're here?" asked Lukian, scratching the back of his neck, feeling uneasy about this mission just as much now as when Brooks assigned it to them.

"Because we have to be," Roi said contemptuously. "Plus, if the target is a no-show, there are plenty of hotties in there we could take home with us. Mmm, fun times. Want to double-team any?"

"Stop talking to me," replied Lukian, staying calm, cool, and collected, despite how much he knew Roi was trying to get him going.

"Okay, but I'm right. We're here because it's orders. Orders fucking blow."

The answer wasn't the one he wanted to hear, but it was the truth. They did have to be here. Lukian knew what their mission was, probably better than Roi. He was, after all, first in command. Search, gather intel, and then eliminate the target. The target was what he had a problem with. It had been a long time since he'd been forced to take a woman's life.

He didn't look forward to it now.

Didn't help matters that he seemed to be having a visceral reaction to the target. Fuck, her photo nearly left him laying claim to her. He wasn't sure what was going on, or how his head had gotten so screwed up, but he did know this mission wasn't sitting well with him.

He glanced down at the photo of the auburn-haired girl he'd been carrying in his back pocket. Her large green eyes had haunted him since he'd first been given the assignment. He knew the rules: don't get attached, don't put a face to the name. He'd broken them both. He'd been fixated on Peren's picture since he'd received it. He silently hoped he wouldn't have to be the one to deliver the killing blow. He'd been doing this kind of work for too long and was too good at it to let this one get to him.

A small sedan pulled into the parking lot, and the hair on the back of Lukian's neck began to rise, his body going on high alert, his senses wild. He sniffed the air and caught a scent he'd not smelled before, but one he felt he knew — somehow, on some baser level. The fierce need to kill anything he deemed threatening to the scent's owner came over him. He wanted to kill anyone and anything near the vehicle, assuring the safety of its passengers.

One in particular.

It was her.

He knew it deep in his bones. A low warning growl began to emanate from him, his beast in agreement with his gut reaction.

Protect the woman.

Roi lifted a brow. "Something you want to share, Captain?"

"No," snapped Lukian, his gaze on the vehicle he knew without a shadow of a doubt held the target. He watched as a tiny woman with ink-black hair and tanned skin opened the car door. He looked at Roi to see how he was holding up, because he knew *this* was Roi's type of woman. If things went badly, they'd be forced to take the friends out as well. Their directive had been only the one target, but they were cleared to do whatever was necessary to eliminate her while securing whatever information it was they thought she had. If that meant additional casualties, then that was fine too.

No, his beast roared within him. It nearly broke free. Sweat beaded on his brow and Lukian reached out, touching Roi's arm lightly. He needed something to ground him. Something to keep him from doing the unthinkable and losing control and shifting.

He knew it then. He couldn't do it. He couldn't do as he'd been directed. Not this time. And he wouldn't let anyone else harm the target either.

She was his.

Mine.

Gathering something close to control, Lukian watched his friend lick his lips again. He knew that Roi was picturing his mouth running all along the little one's body. He squeezed Roi's arm, feeling a bit more like himself and finally able to speak again. "It is best not to think too hard about that one. Trust me, I know. I'm having the same pull to the target. My gut is telling me this whole thing is shit. Brother, I want to protect her, not end her."

"I'm with your gut," said Roi softly. "I want to protect them too."

Lukian watched as the black-haired woman stepped back from the car, pulling the target with her. He slid his fingers over the photo in his hand. Peren, yes, there she was—average height, around five six or so, with anything but an average build. His gaze fell over her white blouse. Its V-neck was low cut and showed the swelling mounds of her breasts. Her tiny waist only made her chest look larger from his vantage point. He wanted to suck on her nipples as he rammed his cock deep within her.

What the hell's your problem? You don't think about targets as sexual objects.

Well, he didn't used to think of targets as sex objects. This one was breaking all his rules. Lukian shifted uncomfortably, trying to get rid of the growing problem between his legs.

Chapter Five

Missy grabbed Peren's arm and led her into the club. The bouncer at the door spent more time flirting with the girls than he did checking their IDs. Melanie stopped and reciprocated his advances as Peren stood silently on the sidelines, the odd feeling of being watched settling over her. She glanced over her shoulder, out the still open door and into the darkness. There was no one there that she could see. Yet she still felt the heavy weight of someone's stare upon her.

When her attention returned to the bouncer, she found him watching her. He wasn't the person who tripped her inner alarms. That much she was sure of. Though, he did keep ogling her, probably hoping he'd somehow manage to get all three of the women to paw him as the women in front of them had.

Not much of a chance of that.

She had little interest in hooking up with a man who probably found a new piece of ass to slip *it* into on a nightly basis. "Pass-around-penis" — the pet name they'd given men who got around — didn't do a thing for her.

This night is going to blow.

Her own lack of interest in her birthday did startle her a bit. It was especially bittersweet for her because it was to be the day that she and Kyle married. It'd been eight months ago that they'd made that decision. He'd proposed to her in the most romantic way. He'd set up a blanket under the stars and had a picnic laid out for them. They'd spent the evening making love and discussing their future. Kyle slipped under her radar and finally swept her off her feet. It had been the day after he'd proposed that he'd gone missing. Eight months hadn't even begun to heal her wounds. No, she still mourned the loss of him daily. Everyone kept telling her that he'd turn up — that he'd gotten cold feet about the wedding and run off to sow his wild oats. Whatever the hell that meant. She knew better. Kyle wasn't like that.

"His grant was approved, he's got you…" She could still hear the police and Kyle's parents defiantly listing the reasons why he'd resurface again. She knew better, though. Kyle would never leave to begin with, not of his own free will. He was too jazzed about his research project for one, and he wouldn't quit talking about marrying her.

"I don't understand why we can't tell everyone that we're engaged right now." The hurt in his voice still echoed in her ear.

"Because you're my professor. Two, my father runs the science department here, remember? You could lose your job over this, Kyle, and you know it. Just give it a few more months, that's all, okay? I'll graduate, your research will be well under way, and no one will be able to stand in our way."

Maybe he wouldn't have stormed off that night if she'd just agreed to his simple demands. Maybe if she'd given in and told the world about their affair, maybe he'd be there with her now. She didn't need someone to tell her he was dead. There was no way that he'd just not come back to her. As much as she hated to admit it, Kyle was dead.

He was dead and gone, and she was stuck trying to plaster a happy face on when all she wanted to do was go home and curl up in bed. Barely past the threshold to the bar, Peren paused, the hair on the back of her neck standing on end, the sense that something was off hitting her hard. She turned, only just catching a glimpse outside as the heavy bar door swung shut. Something was brewing. She knew enough to trust her instincts, and they were telling her that the night was going to totally and utterly blow.

Chapter Six

"Damn, they are...*fine*," Roi said, a cross between a whistle and a growl, his eyes showing signs of shifting colors as he stared across the bar, his focus on the women who had arrived with the target.

Lukian turned to him, regretting bringing him into the damn dump of a bar. He should have left Roi outside sitting in the bushes. His normally even temper was suddenly on the verge of going out of control. He didn't need any of his men making a stupid mistake because they'd let their dicks interfere with their better judgment. There was simply too much at stake now. The women needed to be protected.

Fuck orders.

Lukian let his voice drop, his wolf poking up slightly, reminding Roi who was in charge. "Control your beast. We don't want to have to blow the place up to cover our asses here."

There would be no way to put the horse back in the barn if Roi lost control and shifted forms for all to see. It wasn't as if the I-Ops kept a Fae on speed dial in the event humans needed their memories tweaked. And that skill wasn't something every Fae could even do. If a clean-up team needed called in because Roi turned into a wolf in a bar full of humans, the humans would more than likely meet with untimely, "accidental" deaths. At least that was what the headlines in the papers would read. Lukian's guess would be on a gas line breaking and exploding or some other excuse the government liked to use.

"The only ass I want to cover is hers," Roi said, still fixated on the black-haired girl. Desire rolled off the man and for a second Lukian thought he actually caught the faint scent of mating energy coming from Roi. That couldn't be. Roi wasn't the type of guy who settled down with anyone.

Lukian wondered if she was the woman he'd communicated back and forth with on the computer. She'd seemed nice enough and very intent on seeing Peren happy. A stab of guilt hit him again. Why was this mission getting to him so bad? Why was he ready to throw away everything he'd worked so hard for on a woman he didn't even know?

Mine, his inner voice pushed once more. If he didn't get a grip, it would be Roi having to restrain him to avoid Lukian shifting in front of a bar full of humans.

He watched the girls find a table. Peren's expression made him want to go to her and hold her. For a split second he'd witnessed pure sadness overcoming her and he hated it. Hated knowing she was upset.

"I need a drink," said Roi, clenching his fists, the cords in his neck popping as he clearly struggled to gain control of himself and his wolf.

Lukian would have offered reassuring words, but he was in the same boat. He nodded, a drink sounded perfect. "Better make mine a double."

He had to force himself to look only in the direction of the bar and not at Peren. As they reached the bar, Lukian caught the eye of the bartender. The middle-aged man did a double-take and then tossed his hand towel over his shoulder as he approached. He nodded his head to Lukian. "What can I get you and your buddy?"

"Whiskey," answered Roi, putting his palms on the top of the bar and stretching his fingers. "The whole bottle and a bottle for *my buddy*."

The bartender stared at them from unsure eyes before shrugging and grabbing them each a bottle of whiskey. Roi slid more than enough money to cover the tab across the bar top and then grabbed a bottle for himself. He faced Lukian and began to chug.

Lukian took his bottle, nodded a thanks to the bartender, and did the same. The liquid tickled the back of his throat on the way down, helping him to gain something close to control over his beast once more. As shifters, the men had metabolisms that were vastly different from a human's. A bottle of whiskey wouldn't get them drunk. It would take the edge off their moods, but it wouldn't get them shit-faced by any means.

Roi clutched his bottle. "This is so fucked up, isn't it?"

Lukian wanted to disagree, but knew better than to try. Roi was right. This mission was all kinds of fucked up. The plan had been a simple one. Lure the women to them at the bar, slip into the girls' world undetected, and eliminate the target and then vanish, never to be seen by any of these people again. Peren would hardly be the first person the government had sent him to eliminate. Yes, she was the first female, but that didn't explain the feelings he was having for her. And it didn't explain away why every ounce of his being wanted to scratch the mission and wrap her in his arms.

Focus on the mission.

"Alpha, this is Bravo. Do you read?" He touched his earpiece and spoke softly, looking at Roi in the process who had resorted to chugging his bottle of whiskey.

The rest of the team confirmed their locations, each one responding in his earpiece. Everything was going according to plan, yet it seemed off. Too easy even. Contact information had been handed to his team, as had information on setting up a meeting with the women under the guise of dates. The more Lukian thought on it, the more it twisted at his gut.

"Brother," said Roi, reaching for Lukian's bottle, his own empty. "I might need yours."

Lukian handed it over, his gaze moving in Peren's direction. She had a fake smile plastered to her face, her eyes screaming in pain. She was hurting inside but putting on a brave face.

Roi set the bottle on the bar. "Lukian, look at me."

Confused, Lukian tipped his head, glancing at Roi.

Roi bent, putting his body between Lukian's and everyone else. "Your eyes shifted colors."

"Shit."

"Yeah, shit is right."

Concentrating, Lukian caged his inner beast, thankful Roi was with him. He had no natural-born brothers and Roi had filled that void. Now, they were brothers in every sense of the word. The DNA manipulation had finally been successful and without any ill-timed side effects as had plagued the Immortal Ops program for years prior to Lukian signing on to help. Lukian's assistance and the tireless efforts of several scientists who had been newer to the experiments and who had hated what they saw happening, changed the program for the better. Lukian had even befriended a few of the humans who had helped to turn it all around. Though, he'd lost contact with them nearly twenty or so years ago.

He regretted that. Regretted letting the few human relationships he had developed go by the wayside, but seeing them had served as a reminder of the program's failures—both those prior to his arrival and the ones that happened after he'd signed on. The failures that had resulted in broken leftovers. The men who didn't take fully to the supernatural DNA that had been introduced to them. The Outcasts as they'd been named. And there had been many.

A pang of guilt washed over Lukian. Prior to his full cooperation in the experiments, and before he permitted the government to draw samples from him and use them in the stabilization of the compounds given to the men, so many had either died or been left in conditions where death was often preferable. Some managed to make it out the other side somewhat whole and sane. Though the government hadn't agreed. They thought the men too broken to go on. The Outcasts had been gathered and put in central living quarters for their own good. At least, that was the bullshit line he'd been fed. Lukian had a lot of regrets, most notably that he was now and would forever be a pawn, a killing machine, the government's play toy. Had he really helped mankind by sharing his secret? He wasn't sure yet.

"You going to be all right?" asked Roi.

With a shaky breath, Lukian responded, "Yes."

"Then should we get this show on the

road?"

"Move in, Lance. It's time we learned more about these young ladies," he said slowly into his comm unit. "No harm to any of them yet, understood?"

"Roger that, Captain."

"I'm serious. Do not test me on this."

Lance snorted. "I never would, sir."

Chapter Seven

"Where are they?" Melanie asked, tapping her long, painted, pink nails on the table. There wasn't a time Peren could remember that Melanie had a hair out of place, and they'd known one another for years.

Often, Peren felt that she was barely keeping her own shit together and didn't have time to worry about things such as manicures and pedicures.

Missy shrugged and looked around the bar. "I don't know. When did they say they'd be here?"

"They should *already* be here," responded Melanie.

Great. They were up to something.

Missy glanced over Peren's shoulder and smiled wildly. "I spy something blond and sexy with my little brown eyes."

Both Peren and Melanie turned to see a tall, buzz-cut blond coming toward their table. The man had a certain Nordic appeal to him. He reminded Peren of a god of old or mythical being. Not some random guy frequenting a tiny roadside bar that seemed to be held together by dirt and who knew what else. There was something about the man. Something that made her take more notice than she normally would. The feeling of unease returned, this time making the tiny hairs on her arms rise. The urge to flee the area, and to waste no time doing it, hit her hard, setting her even more on edge.

Not that she needed any help.

"You Melanie?" the blond man asked.

Melanie nodded. A Cheshire cat smile crept over her face as she stood and offered him her hand. "You must be Lance. I was starting to think you weren't coming," she said, her lip puckered out in a semi-pout. She did a very on-purpose yet casual toss of her white-blonde locks over her shoulder. And just like that the blond god named Lance fell for the blonde supermodel, hook, line, and sinker.

She does it to the best of 'em, buddy.

Mel had a way of getting men to eat out of her hand. Peren wasn't sure if it was Mel's demeanor or if it was because she really did look like a supermodel.

Ah, to be five-ten and blonde…

"I thought you said you were bringing friends?" Melanie's voice managed to be accusatory and sexy all in one fell swoop. It was an art that Peren had started to pick up on though she lacked the skills to pull it off.

Lance kissed Melanie's hand gently. "They're at the bar. What would everyone like to drink?" His light-blue gaze came to Peren. It turned cold and icy — making fear creep up her spine. She sat back in her seat from the weight of his stare.

"Nothing…water," she managed, suddenly uneasy but unsure why.

"I'll have a Long Island Iced Tea and Missy will take a beer. She's hardcore like that. Thanks, Lance," said Melanie, as sultry as ever. "Hurry back."

The man was only a few feet from their table when Melanie giggled. "I am so taking a ride on that dick tonight."

Missy snorted and rolled her eyes. "What a

shocker."

Peren even had to laugh a little. "Tell me you're not expecting Missy and me to ride his friends."

"I would tell you that," said Melanie with a wink. "But that would be a lie."

Chapter Eight

Lukian waited as Lance walked toward them. The guy was focused, no surprise there. Lance was the go-to boy. Lance nodded at them, but Lukian waited for him to get closer before acknowledging him.

"Confirmation on the target, sir, and the women don't suspect anything," Lance said, but something in his voice hitched. "Sir. If I may."

"Go ahead," said Lukian, his gut churning at the idea the mission was unfolding. "Speak your mind."

"Something seem off to you too, Captain?" asked Lance, eyeing him carefully. "When do we follow through on the original order? When do we eliminate the target?"

Lukian's stomach dropped. When he sensed something was wrong, that generally meant they had a problem. A big one.

He looked to Lance. "Something is totally off with this."

Lance nodded, paling slightly. "My spider

senses are all over the place."

"Spider senses? You're a cat shifter, not a spider shifter."

Roi shook his head. "Old-timer."

Putting his hand out, Lukian caught his best friend by the arm. "Roi, abort the operation," he said, his breathing becoming erratic. "Tell the rest of the men and meet me at the table in five minutes. We need to know more about the target. This doesn't feel right at all."

"Really?" Roi's eyes widened. He felt it too, Lukian was sure of it. "Bravo, this is Alpha-Dog-Two. Abort mission and stand down," said Roi, into his comm unit, relief shining on his face.

Lance moved alongside Lukian as he made his way to the table. The closer Lukian got to the target, the harder it was to breathe. His heart felt as though it would beat out of his chest. What the hell was wrong with him? Why was this woman having this effect on him? She was hardly the first pretty girl he'd been around in his long life. She wouldn't be the last.

So why her?

Why now?

Why this mission?

So many questions, and the only answer he had was that she was not to be harmed. Fuck orders.

Chapter Nine

"Yummy," Melanie said as she watched Lance returning to the table with his tall, dark, and handsome friend in tow. Each man had drinks in their hands.

The way the newcomer stared at Peren left little room for doubt. He was the guy they were hoping to fix her up with. And his expression said he wouldn't take no for an answer. The man screamed alpha male. Every step he took reaffirmed his dominance.

Emotions welled and seemed at odds with one another as one part of her brain said go for it, he's hot, and the other screamed her heart wasn't ready yet. And all the while her instincts kept pushing her to run—to get away from the area, that danger was close.

Was it the men she was afraid of?

No.

Something else.

Buried memories of a past she'd wanted to keep tucked away began to creep in on her. She thought of her time with a fortune-teller, on her tenth birthday, when her father had rented a circus for her and only her. On that night and that night alone, no other patrons had been there. Only Peren, her mother, and Peren's nanny. Oh, the fun they'd first had, riding rides, eating junk food, and laughing together. When Peren's mother decided to visit the fortune-teller's tent, Peren's gut had twisted and she'd felt the urge to flee—to get far from the area. She'd ignored that push then. That inner alarm sounding and telling her something was wrong and off.

She'd regretted ignoring it every day since.

The same feeling of unease she'd felt that long-ago day moved over her now. She wanted to run. To get away. But no, that couldn't happen again—could it? Everyone had told her she'd imagined all of it. That seeing a man turn into a wolf wasn't possible—that watching the people she loved die in front of her had caused hallucinations, caused her mind to break under the weight of it all.

She'd not imagined the look of horror on the fortune-teller's face when she'd touched

Peren or the horrible words she'd shouted, about Peren being an abomination. She hadn't imagined fleeing from the tent, a scared, impulsive ten-year-old girl, running out into the night, wanting to be away from the horrid things the woman had continued to yell.

And no matter what anyone had said, she had not imagined the beast that came out of the darkness, in the woods surrounding the circus, its mouth full of blood, smelling of death. There had been no child's play at hand when it had caught her by the ankle and sunk its teeth into her leg, tearing at her flesh, making her scream. No play of light when she'd felt a surge of cold, hard energy lash out of her, hitting the creature with such force that it flew off her. And later, after she'd woken in the hospital, her father at her bedside and the police nearby, everyone's faces aghast, she had not imagined overhearing their hushed whispers as they spoke of the mutilated bodies of the circus workers, the fortune-teller, and Peren's mother and nanny being discovered. They could call it anything they wanted—a pack of wild animals attacking, a fluke of nature—but she knew the truth. Whatever had attacked them wasn't natural, and it wasn't simply an animal.

It was so much more.

Wild animals didn't morph into people. She knew what she'd seen back then, and she would never forget how she'd felt before it all happened.

The same way she felt now.

The men continued to approach, and she thought she'd actually get up and run, but as the man with the blond guy moved in closer, Peren realized it wasn't him she was afraid of. He radiated something that almost pushed away the worry and dread that was assailing her. But if it wasn't him, then what was causing her unease, her fear?

"Where'd the other guy go?" Missy asked, glancing right past the man with Lance.

"What other guy?" asked Peren, having seen just two men.

Missy kept staring off into the distance toward the entrance of the bar. "The other guy with black hair. He was with them near the bar."

Peren couldn't focus fully as she looked around, trying hard to figure out what was causing the extreme anxiety settling over her. This was far more than nerves over a blind date ambush. She'd experienced true fear and horror, and she knew it wasn't far from her now.

Lance and the newcomer came to a stop before the table of girls and began to hand out drinks. The tall, dark and clearly-in-charge male handed Peren her drink. The second their fingers brushed, heat rushed over her, taking her already erratic emotional state and pushing it over the edge. She needed air. Needed space. Needed to get away from the man's piercing gaze.

Standing, she drew Missy's attention. Her friend grabbed her hand. "You okay?"

"No," whispered Peren, her gaze locking on the man. As his tongue darted out and over his lip, the apex of her thighs pooled with moisture. There were too many conflicting emotions hitting her at once. Annoyance with her friends for clearly going against her wishes and trying to set her up, frustration for being sexually attracted to the man they'd brought, and fear of something—she just wasn't sure what. It all bubbled over into an irrational outburst.

"What's wrong?" asked Missy.

"What's wrong?" repeated Peren. "I'll tell you what's wrong. You two can't seem to stop meddling in things you don't understand. I don't want to be here. I don't want to be fixed up with another one of your ideas of the perfect man. Contrary to popular belief, we all don't want to get fucked by the first thing that shows any interest in us. Besides, testosterone-driven sex machines with little to no brains do not appeal to me."

"Now that's a shame. For a minute there, I thought I actually had a shot. But I can't do much about the testosterone thing. Sort of comes with the territory when you're dealing with me, sweetheart. As for showing an interest in you...that shouldn't be too hard. I should take offense that you think all men with muscles have no brains. I *should*, but I won't."

Peren turned to see who had spoken to her. Her gaze fell on the tall man who stood with Lance. As much as she hated to admit it, he was breathtaking, with his wide shoulders and head of shoulder-length black hair. Its waviness rivaled her own, although her hair was at least a foot longer than his. She noticed right off the bat that he had a tiny scar above his right eyebrow and that his eyelashes were blacker than hers. The thick lashes drew attention to his royal blue gaze. The blue was so intense that it couldn't be natural. She was sure they were contacts.

You're sensing danger and focusing on some guy's eyes. Ohmygod, you're now a brainless dumbass too, she thought, and then took a deep, calming breath. *There is nothing to be scared of. Your nerves are just shot. Go home and rest.*

The beginning of a five o'clock shadow softened what could easily be taken as too masculine a face. His jaw tightened as she took a step back. He wasn't pleased that she hadn't taken an instant interest in him. *Oh well.* It wasn't like she hadn't given any thought to having sex with him

I'm grieving, not dead. And I'm also leaving.

Peren turned and went quickly toward the club door. She heard her friends calling out to her but didn't turn to them. They could busy themselves with their new finds all night. She hoped they'd be too sore to walk after spending the night getting ridden hard. It'd serve them right. No fear of that for her. No, she'd be sleeping alone again, because she was going home. Mr. Tall-Dark-and-Sexy would have to be reserved only for her dreams.

Thankfully, I've got fingers. And, if need be, the will to use them.

Chapter Ten

"Shit," the tall blonde girl said as she watched the target leave. She turned to run after her but found Lance holding her arm like a good soldier, making sure the woman stayed in place. Having the other woman running out while there was a target painted on her back wasn't good at all.

"Peren," said the blonde woman, looking worried.

It wouldn't do any of them any good if all the women were scattered to the winds. No. His men could watch over these two while he went after the one who made his dick hard enough to hammer nails with.

"I'll go. Maybe I could throw up a white flag or something," Lukian said, smiling widely at the girls. Not wanting to alarm them, though he knew the situation was serious. If a kill order was on Peren, there was a reason for it. That meant she wasn't safe. Didn't help that he wanted to bed her in a way he'd never done another. And that meant she *really* wasn't safe at all.

Not even from him, sadly.

The girls exchanged glances then nodded.

Leave it to women to trust a cold-blooded killing machine with their friend's life. He glanced back at Roi and nodded in the direction of the door before leaving. Roi gave him a thumbs-up as he left to retrieve Peren.

Lukian hit the outside and took a deep breath. The scents of the night filled his lungs. He craved the night air and running free in wolf form. Tonight he craved something else too, and it was headed down the darkened street, apparently planning to walk all the way home, rather than use a car.

Stubborn woman.

Damn, he wanted her even more after she'd scolded him and then stormed out. He liked a challenge, and Peren was proving to be one. He just had to keep her safe long enough to figure out just how much of one she was capable of being.

Lukian took off in a slow run in the direction of her scent. Even in the darkness of the night, he could see her clearly. His night vision was excellent. It had to be. The blood of the wolf that ran through him would not have it any other way.

He caught up to Peren with ease and slowed his pace, reading her thoughts, mildly amused with her opinion of him in the process. She was definitely attracted to him but conflicted. She was also doing her best to fight off her feelings of fear. He wanted to tell her she had nothing to worry about, but explaining how he knew she was afraid of anything at all wasn't a conversation he wanted to have. Besides, he was reading way more from her than he did others. Reading her thoughts was easy for him. Most humans weren't too difficult for him to eavesdrop on, but Peren was like an open book to him. That caught him a little off-guard.

He stopped and put his hands up in the air slowly as she shot a dirty look over her shoulder at him. "I come in peace."

Her full lips curved into a smile so white that she lit up the night, causing his insides to lurch forward. His cock wanted to be in her so badly that he wondered if he could control himself. He was far too old to be behaving as if he were still a young pup. He was experienced now and wise enough to be able to control his erections at will, or at least he had thought so prior to meeting Peren.

The wind caught her long skirt and blew it up. Shiny black leather boots that ran up to her knee showed through. He waited for a better glimpse at what kind of panties she wore under her skirt, but the wind refused to help out any longer.

Just as well. He'd probably jump on her right here and now.

This target of his, Peren, stirred things in him that hadn't existed in over a century. He watched her take a wider stance, one a person with defensive skills would assume. She was ready to try to protect herself. It hit him then that if all had gone according to plan, she'd be dead already, so her instincts were good, but so were his.

Chapter Eleven

Peren tried but failed to wipe the smile from her face as the man from the bar stood near her, his hands in the air, looking like a fool with a lopsided grin on his face. She wanted to be angry that he'd followed her, but something about him made her grin. "What do you want?"

He gave her a large smile and shrugged, his shirt pulling against his muscles as he did. "I'm not sure, maybe to know that I wasn't what chased you off. That could leave lasting effects on a man's ego."

I'll just bet you've got ego problems.

No, he looked like the type who was incredibly comfortable in his own skin. She thought about how comfortable she'd be skin to skin with him too and shook her head.

Cut it out. You don't sleep around. You leave that up to Melanie. She's good at it.

"I'm Lukian, and you must be Peren," the man said, extending his large hand out to her. She took a small step forward and grabbed it quickly. A spark of energy flew between them.

The same thing had happened long ago, the night she'd had her fortune told, the night her entire world turned upside down. All the fear and dread she'd been sensing since arriving at the bar hit her in a wave that nearly took her legs out from under her. There was no way she could push down or ignore the urge to flee. It coursed through her every fiber.

For a split second Lukian appeared confused, and then an expression settled over his face that told her he was fully expecting her to panic and run. But how did he know? She wasn't going to wait around to find out.

Distance.

She needed distance between her and the feeling of danger—whatever the hell was causing it. Peren didn't run back in the direction of the bar and her friends. Instinct drove her away, as if something deep down was telling her to avoid taking the trouble to them and laying it at their feet. She gave in, turned, and ran as fast as she possibly could, her past blurring with her present, the fear all-consuming.

She hit the edge of the woods and never skipped a beat. She knew she didn't have that good of a lead on him and that he'd catch up if she dared to stop. A limb scraped her cheek, and she whimpered, pushing onward wildly.

It's just a scratch, definitely not worth dying over.

She could see the forest in her mind, even though she could not see her hand before her face in the darkness. The same type of darkness that had blanketed her that fateful night when she was ten. That same feeling of fear and of being hunted. *Not again* — her mind raced as she ran. She thought back to the night of her tenth birthday. Every fear and bit of pain she'd felt then washed over her, giving her the strength to push forward, to draw on whatever thing lived inside her — whatever thing that made her an abomination. Whatever thing that had saved her life that night long ago.

Chapter Twelve

What the hell is she? Lukian's mind raced as his feet moved quickly under him. He was faster than any human could hope to be. Yet this tiny woman was managing to outrun him. She couldn't weigh more than a buck o' five, yet she made him work to catch her. Perhaps he'd been wrong to abort the mission. Apparently, he was dealing with more than just a pretty face. And more than just a human.

No, his inner beast roared. He wasn't wrong. She was not to be harmed. The beast was very clear on that much.

Stopping, he sniffed the air, the wolf in him clawing at his gut, demanding to be set free to hunt her. It didn't want to harm her. It wanted to own her, mark her, make her his.

Mine.

The word thrashed around in his head, jumbled with her thoughts, still assailing him in a way no other's ever had. Lukian did his best to hone in on her location, but somehow she blocked it from him. The only others he'd ever encountered who were able to do such a thing were trained operatives. He'd never met a civilian able to pull off such a feat. Had she been trained? Had she been recruited to join an elite team too? Perhaps she was from a unit similar to his own? Maybe she was with Paranormal Security and Intelligence (PSI), another branch of government that stayed hidden from humans but operated to help police supernaturals. But if she was, an elimination order would not have been issued to the I-Ops. No. PSI handled their own affairs. A sobering thought struck him. Maybe she didn't work for the same side he did. Maybe she was with the enemy.

No!

His wolf nearly won the struggle for freedom, its insistence she was not the enemy making him sway as he fought for control. He fixated on her scent, sweet vanilla with hints of flowers. He took a moment to catch his bearings and figure his exact location. They'd scouted the area enough for him to know where he was and what she was doing. She was headed back to the road.

Smart girl.

He heard her rustling off to his left, and a slow smile crept over his face.

Not smart enough, though.

He leaped up and over a rock to a ledge, hoping that the higher vantage point would allow him to not only see her but possibly be able to surprise her from above as well. It took a moment for him to calm his wolf side enough to focus fully on Peren, but when he did, he heard her pulse racing. His own sped to match, syncing with hers as if he were afraid. As attuned as he was to her, Lukian's breathing fell in line with hers as well. In all his years, he'd never had such a thing occur.

What was she?

And why did he care so much?

You know why, he thought, shaking his head, hoping to banish the thought. No. It couldn't be. She couldn't be his mate. The odds of that were too high. And he'd long ago given up any hope of ever finding the one person created for him. Yet there was no denying the pull to her or the fact his wolf was obsessed with her.

Her thoughts hit him hard once more. Images of a carnival of sorts flashed in his mind. He saw a young girl, no more than ten, holding the hand of a woman as they entered a tent. Drapes of red hung from all directions in the tent, and a circular table sat in the center. At the table was a woman wearing many necklaces, and a silk scarf tied around her head. Large hoop earrings adorned the woman's ears, and they jingled as the woman leaned, looking at a crystal ball on the table. The young girl was fascinated by the earrings at first before her attention went to the woman — the fortuneteller.

Lukian realized then the flashes were memories of Peren's. That she was somehow sharing them with him, though he wasn't even sure she realized she was doing it. Crouching, he lowered his head and put a hand on the ground to steady himself as her memories continued to wash over him.

The fortuneteller's head had snapped up.

Her dark gaze whipping to the young girl, her eyes going milky white suddenly, scaring the girl, right before the woman proceeded to yell.

Abomination.

The word sent a chill down his spine.

Scenes from the past continued to play out in his mind, the emotions tied to them feeling as if they were his own. It was nearly impossible to stay removed from it all—to feel nothing. He wanted to reach through the memories and rip the woman to shreds. The very moment the idea struck him, another vision came, this one of a clawed, fur-covered arm doing just that—killing the woman.

Butchering her and the others around her before giving chase. It wanted something. What?

Lukian nearly toppled over as it hit him. The beast had wanted Peren. It had hunted her, its intent unclear, but one thing was for certain. It was a shifter, not a normal animal, and it had sampled her—tasted her flesh and blood.

His gaze snapped open, and he looked out into the darkness, the sound of his pulse beating in his ears, temporarily blocking him from hearing anything else. Peren had survived a werewolf bite as a child, and she'd witnessed deaths at the hands of a shifter.

Oh God, she was attacked by one of us, a fellow shifter.

His heart sank with sadness. Here he was chasing this woman, making her relive the same feelings of horror she'd experienced as a child. He wasn't so old that he couldn't remember what it was like to be a child, but he'd been born this way. Born able to change into a wolf.

A shudder ran through his veins. He couldn't imagine running into a werewolf at such a young age and then having it attack. His heart broke for Peren, filling him with an overwhelming need to find and protect her. Someone wanted her dead, and he was supposed to be the man to do it. He knew that would never happen. He'd find out who had issued the hit order, and he'd tear them limb from limb for daring to think harm should befall his woman.

My woman?

Lukian gasped at the thought. He caught the scent of his own kind near, and confusion knitted his brow. His men had been trained to mask their scents. Mask who and what they were. Why were they suddenly being so careless? What had happened?

Another thought struck him.

Maybe what he smelled wasn't his men at all, but other shifters. If that was the case, they were there for one thing and one thing only.

Peren.

Tapping his transmitter, he looked around, trying to discern what direction the shifters were in. Their scent blanketed the area, as if they were everywhere at once all of a sudden. "Ops, status report."

It was Green who responded. "Bravo is holding at station one, in stand-down mode. The rest of Alpha is still together and in the club, Captain."

Shit.

That was what he was afraid of. Something else was out here in the night with them.

Someone wanted her dead enough to bother sending additional hitters. His team wasn't cheap, and sending in backups meant that someone with a lot of power and money was backing this. Lukian tried to imagine what Peren could have done that would make someone so adamant about seeing her life come to an end, but he came up empty-handed. The hows and whys were irrelevant. There was no way he'd let any harm come to her.

He scanned the woods for a sign of her and then waited. Within seconds she came running toward him.

It's now or never.

Chapter Thirteen

Peren continued to run, unsure where she was going or why she was running. All she knew was danger was close and she had to keep moving. She also knew that heading back to the bar would be bad — that she would take trouble right to the doorstep of her best friends in all the world. Two women she considered to be sisters to her. There was no way she would drop the devil at their feet.

Each step she took brought with it memories of her tenth birthday. She tried to push it all from her mind, but the harder she tried, the more she felt the same as she had when she was young. The same fear, the same feeling that a beast was on her heels, and the same fear she'd felt when it had caught up with her long enough to sink its teeth into her.

The trees over her head shuffled, and there was no reaction time as the heavy weight of a man fell onto her. He knocked her to the ground, sending pain shooting up and through her head. She tried to scream, but his hand clasped over her mouth.

"They will hear you," Lukian said softly in her ear. She tried to scream again. She wanted him off her and hoped that everyone in the world would hear. She bit down on his hand and he tightened his grip on her. "Shit, I'm trying to help you. Something, someone, is coming for you—" A loud howl interrupted him.

Peren's body tightened under his as terror filled her veins. Lukian hadn't made the noise. If he wasn't what she was running from, then what was it? The realization that she knew that sound and had heard it before hit her hard, leaving her sinking against Lukian's powerful body. She'd heard the same howl on her tenth birthday. It was forever embedded in her brain. She would never forget it. The only person who had believed her had been Kyle, and he was gone.

Whatever had attacked her that night long ago was back.

Lukian held tight to her and pulled her to her feet, twisting her around to look at him.

She met his eyes with tears glistening in her own. She wasn't one to cry in front of others, but the terror gripping her body was too great for her to deal with alone. The look on Lukian's face told her he wasn't about to abandon her, regardless of the beastly noises around them.

Brave man.

Another high-pitched wolf howl sounded from their left. Her body went rigid with fear. She resisted the urge to shriek and stared at this tall, mysterious man who claimed to be on her side. Could she trust him? Did she have a choice?

A growl came from their right this time. Lukian turned first, putting his body in front of hers in a protective manner. He whispered something to himself that she couldn't make out, but sounded vaguely like Alpha something or other. Was he talking to her? If so, he wasn't making any sense.

He reached into the back of his tan pants and pulled out a handgun. She scanned the contours of it and recognized it for what it was —military issue. Her father had spent the greater part of his scientific career working for the military. He'd been out of the business since she'd been born, but had never lost his interest in all things military. He loved to quiz her on interesting bits of trivia and to test her hand-to-hand combat training. He raised her much like he would have had she been a boy. She'd always felt as if she'd let him down when she'd chosen art school over the armed services. Regardless, she knew enough of weapons to recognize several on sight, and the one Lukian was carrying was hardly a peashooter.

Lukian pushed her body behind his even more, acting as a barrier between her and whatever was surrounding them. No fear showed on him, and his braveness in the face of the unknown helped to calm her to a degree. Though a pang of curiosity lit in her. Why wasn't he afraid? Ordinary people would have been afraid. Peren was hardly what anyone would label typical, and she was terrified. She raked her gaze down Lukian's back, her eyes adjusting more and more to the darkness, allowing her to see with ease. The man before her was a well-oiled fighting machine. How had she missed that before?

Ordinary, my ass! she thought, shaking her head, her focus on his backside.

Ordinary, everyday citizens didn't run around carrying military-issue handguns with them. Nope, Lukian was definitely hiding something.

Reaching back, he took hold of her arm with one hand and heat raced over her flesh. She gasped, the sensation that he was composed solely of static energy rushing through her for the briefest of moments. It faded, but the draw to him didn't. That only strengthened. She tensed but allowed him to move her backward gradually. His hand brushed over her right breast in the process and her nipples hardened instantaneously. Without thought, she touched his muscular arm. He flexed under the weight of her fingers.

Typical male reaction.

He inched his hand farther around her, pressing her to his back while his hand rested firmly on her backside. The tighter the grip on her ass got, the more damp her inner thighs became.

Now is not the time to be thinking of banging the hot guy. Now is the time to think about surviving.

She did her best to shake the naughty thoughts from her head. They left, just in time to be replaced by thoughts of death and destruction as more howls followed. She almost wanted the horny thoughts back instead. A flash of fur seemed to come right at them. Peren cried out, fear gripping her in its hold like an iron fist. Lukian never so much as flinched as he took aim and fired, scoring a direct shot to the forehead of a ginormous animal.

It was no ordinary wolf, not unless someone had figured out a way to breed wolves with horses—the thing was that big. It fell to the ground with a thud. The animal rights advocate in her didn't even cause a fuss, as the inner certainty that whatever the beast was, it wasn't natural, settled over her. It was like the one she'd seen when she was ten. And she'd bet all the money in the world that it wasn't just a wolf. That it could be a man if it wanted to be. A brief moment of relief nearly overcame her when she sensed something else close to them. Two more giant wolves leapt out of the darkness at them.

Lukian fired at one, scoring another hit, but not before whatever it was crashed into him. Lukian's weapon scattered into the darkness, vanishing under brush just as the second of the attackers went directly for the back of Lukian's neck.

The training her father had started to put her through after the events of her tenth birthday kicked in, directing her actions as if she were on autopilot. She kicked at the wolf, striking its side. The sound of bones breaking rent the air, accompanied quickly by the wolf's yelps. It fell off course. Lukian was safe for the time being. Though that was short-lived as the beast snarled, snapping its jaws and nearly catching Lukian in the process. She made a move to kick it again, but Lukian shoved her with just enough force to move her out of the wolf's reach. The beast shrank back for a moment before making a play for her. Lukian snatched the wolf by its throat, out of midair. The action looked like something out of a movie. It was surreal seeing that much power in a man as he snapped the animal's neck with one hand and very little in the way of effort.

It wasn't over. She didn't need to hear more howls or growls to know there were others around them. Others who wanted to kill. Lukian twisted, his blue gaze moving over her, his poker face cracking slightly, showing relief. In that second she knew the relief was for her—that she wasn't harmed. Unable to help herself, Peren lifted a hand, wanting to make contact with the man. Wanting to feel his flesh against hers. Some inner force driving her to want to be sure he too was okay. His gaze went to her hand, and in that very second a large mass burst free from the bushes nearest them and pummeled into Lukian, sending him hurtling to the ground. She grabbed at the snarling mass on Lukian of what seemed to be part human and part beast in an attempt to pull it from him. Just as her fingers nearly connected with it, pain shot through her head as something snatched her up and off her feet by her hair.

Chapter Fourteen

Lukian rolled onto his stomach and brought the half-changed werewolf around with him. He struck out, catching its jaw. His fingers burned for the change. His body wanted to be allowed to go to wolf form for the battle. He knew he could take them, all of them, as a wolf. He also knew the act of shape-shifting in front of Peren would send her screaming to her death if she saw him become what she feared most. He resisted the burning need to allow his wolf free and fought in human form.

He brought his knee up hard and caught the half-wolf in the gut. It lurched back. Putting his hands over his head, Lukian touched the hard earth with his palms and thrust himself upward in one fluid motion.

"The cavalry is here, Captain. Take cover." He heard the voice of Jon—the team's sniper—in his earpiece.

Good.

His team would assist and help make short

work of the rogues around them, allowing Lukian to focus on Peren and her safety. He kicked, sent the half-wolf flying high into the air, and spun, looking for Peren. She was no longer near him. She wasn't anywhere that he could see or smell. His heart lodged in his throat and his hand went to his transponder.

"Jon, hold your fire. Hold your fire!"

Lukian dropped down, looking at the dirt beneath him. Tracking came naturally to him. It was in his blood. He'd been born to be a hunter and he let his instincts take over. He sniffed the air, running his fingers over the imprints in the ground from Peren's boots. A set of large footprints was next to hers, matching the dragging pattern she'd left step for step. A shifter had her and she'd not gone willingly. His beast roared within him, wanting to be free. He almost let it, but his fear of not being able to rein it again seemed justified. It had never been this forceful, this insistent, and he wasn't sure he'd be able to put the horse back in the barn once it was set free.

If anyone harms my woman, they will die.

"Captain?" Green's voice came over the comm.

Lukian ignored his fellow teammate, his attention on Peren and tracking her. It was all he could do to keep his beast caged. He couldn't focus on anything else. Not when she was missing.

Her screams slashed through the darkness, stabbing at him.

I'm coming, baby, hold on.

He ran fast and hard. His boots gave him the traction he needed to scale up the side of a rock wall to shave time off his pursuit. He hit the road just as headlights splashed over him. A van squealed to a stop in front of him. The side door slid open, revealing Jon and Wilson, both men dressed in black from head to toe. Lukian met Jon's confused amber gaze and struggled to get his breathing under control. "Jon, they took her... I lost the trail. We have to find her! We have to protect her!"

Wilson moved forward, nudging Jon out of the way. "But, Captain, aren't we supposed to eliminate her? We should be sending whoever did it a thank-you note for making our life a hell of a lot easier, if you ask me."

Lukian grabbed hold of Wilson and ripped him out of the vehicle. His left hand changed, morphing into partial wolf form. He held his claws under the wererat's chin. "I didn't ask you, and if they hurt her, I will kill you. Am I clear?"

"Sir, I believe we understand your position on this matter now. If you would please be so kind as to put Wilson down, we can begin combing the area for signs of her," Green said from the driver's seat, ever the voice of reason.

Green was well known for his levelheadedness. Lukian nodded a quick thanks at him and set Wilson back on his feet. He knew he'd shaken the guy up. He hadn't meant to, but the thought of someone hurting Peren sickened him.

Chapter Fifteen

Peren clawed at the thing dragging her through the woods. She tried desperately to unhook its clawed, furry fingers from the back of her head, and it pulled her along. She beat at its arm to no avail. The more she tried to reach up and behind her to get it off her, the harder its grip on her hair was. Tears streamed down her cheeks, born of fear, adrenaline, and pain. She knew without a shadow of a doubt that whatever had her was like the thing she'd encountered when she was ten. She'd seen what that had been capable of. She'd witnessed its brutality and savageness firsthand.

She was going to die, and her death was going to be horrific and painful.

The monster dragging Peren by her hair let go long enough for her to fall to the ground. She tried to pick herself up again but knew she was past her limits. It struck the side of her face, and her head snapped backward as pain exploded through her body. For a moment, she wondered if the monster had killed her. Was this death?

Darkness.

A feeling of falling endlessly.

When she felt like her head was about to burst, her vision swirling with multicolored dots, she knew she was still alive. Death couldn't possibly still hurt, could it?

Hot breath blew down on her cheek. She tried to open her eyes to see what was next to her, but the strike she'd taken kept her relatively immobile. Something rough like sandpaper and slightly damp moved over her cheek.

A tongue. It's a tongue.

Her mind tried to process the information as fast as it came in, but it was too much, too soon. She wanted to vomit and scream.

"I'm going to enjoy this," a deep raspy voice whispered in her ear.

A scared whimper was all she managed in response, and she hated herself for that. Hated how weak she was compared to whatever had her in its grip and was toying with her. She was the mouse, it the cat—or in this case, wolf.

"It's time to collect the debt owed to me," it said, its voice sounding slightly more human and oddly familiar.

A huge weight dropped on her. She struck out, trying to get it off. She heard material ripping and felt the sharp sensation of fingernails being dragged down her side.

"Peren!" Lukian's voice cut through the darkness around her. He couldn't have sounded more like an angel if he'd tried.

The thing pulled back from her as she cried out for help. Something heavy struck the side of her head. "Luke," she said softly. It was all she could manage to get out before she gave in to the overriding darkness that surrounded her.

*

Lukian ran through the woods, drawing more and more upon his wolf in search of Peren. Jon and Wilson were hot on his trail, moving with inhuman speed as well. Jon whistled, and the men came to a dead stop.

Jon touched Lukian's back. "Captain, do you smell that?"

"What the fuck is that?" asked Wilson, coming to a stop next to Lukian.

"Death," replied Lukian.

Whatever was dead had been so much longer than a few minutes. That was the only thing that kept him somewhat calm. It wasn't Peren. It couldn't be. But it had been human.

Jon moved through the brush and then stepped back out, his face ashen. "Captain, there are three dead hikers piled in a shallow grave there. Looks like someone tried to cover them with whatever they could find that might mask the smell of decaying flesh from shifters."

Wilson lifted a brow. "What the hell is going on?"

Jon cast Lukian a sideways glance and shook his head.

Lukian was about to comment when he heard the muffled sound of a woman's cry. Hope filled him as he recognized Peren's soft scent. He smelled something else too.

Something that made him take pause.

Desire.

It was mixed with so much rage that he knew in an instant the man's intent was to take what he wanted from Peren, consequences be damned.

Like fucking hell.

Twisting, Lukian grabbed an extra weapon from Wilson and took off running.

He felt Peren's fear and then her pain when she received a blow to the head. The muscles in his neck tightened with the anticipation of tearing off the head of the shifter who had hurt her. He heard her whisper his name, or almost his name. She called him Luke. It had been a long time since someone had called him that. The norm now was Captain and had been for decades.

Peren's scent filled the air around him. He was close. Pushing through a large patch of brush, he found her lying on her side, clutching herself in obvious pain. A feeling of failure gripped him. He'd let someone harm her when he had vowed he wouldn't. He scanned the area first for the assailant. The threat was gone.

Now he needed to tend to his woman. He dropped to his knees next to Peren.

She screamed, jerking away from him, breaking any remaining resistance he had to her. "It's me," he murmured. "It's Lukian."

"Luke?" Her tiny hand came out and slipped into his.

Jon and Wilson burst through the bushes, weapons drawn, protecting his back while he saw to *his* Peren.

My Peren?

The words sounded so sweet in his head that for the first time in a long time he had butterflies in his stomach. He scooped her up in his arms and held her close.

Chapter Sixteen

Roi Majors laughed as Missy, the little black-haired one, tried to stop him from putting her in the van. She had pitched one hell of a fit in the bar, demanding to know where her friend was, and why Roi refused to let her leave to search for the girl. Sure, he could have explained it all to the little hottie, but it was more fun watching her get riled up. She was a hellcat, and it turned him on. Everything about the tiny stick of dynamite did. From her small build to her large, expressive brown eyes that reminded him of cat eyes. Though at the moment they were narrowed on him, glaring daggers.

"You're an asshole," she spat, a hand going to her hip.

With a shrug, Roi stepped closer to her. "Yep. That seems to be the general consensus."

"Where is Peren and where in the hell is your buddy? The guy who looks like you."

Roi knew she meant Lukian. Most people assumed they were biological brothers because they did look very similar. "Probably playing hide the salami with your friend. The one with the red hair who threw the temper tantrum and stormed out of the bar."

Missy's nostrils flared and Roi half-expected her to slap him. "You're a pig."

"Asshole or pig," he said clearly. "Pick one."

She crossed her arms under her small, perky breasts. "You're a pig's asshole."

He hadn't been called that before. He grinned. "That's a new one."

"Fits."

"Get in the van," he said, motioning to the vehicle.

She gave him a "not on your life, bucko" look and continued to stand there, her arms crossed.

Damn. She was fucking flawless. His dick was hard simply being near her.

"Now."

"Eat me," she retorted.

He nodded. "Okay, but get in the van first. I'll eat you *out* all fucking night long after that, and you'll enjoy every minute of it."

"That will be hard to do after I rip your tongue out," she snapped.

His cock twitched. He really wanted this woman. "You've got spunk. Now get in the damn van."

"Missy," said the blonde woman, her hand on Lance's arm. "Please. Let's go with them. They said it's important and about Peren."

Missy snorted. "And you believe them? Melanie, rule number one on how to avoid ending up in a crime scene report. Don't get in vans with strange men."

"Lance isn't strange," Melanie said with a huff. "And I trust them."

Roi glanced at Lance, wondering what he'd done to get the blonde to be so easygoing. Whatever it was, Roi needed to borrow it because Missy was hardheaded.

Melanie made a move to step into the van with Lance's assistance, and Missy reached out, grabbed her friend's arm, and tugged. "No way. We aren't going anywhere with you two until you tell us what is going on."

"Missy, stop," protested Melanie, jerking free and getting in the van. Lance followed and grinned at Roi.

"Asshole," Roi whispered under his breath, just loud enough for Lance to hear.

Missy grunted. "I'm not an asshole. You are."

She'd heard him?

How?

The van started, and Roi stared down at the tiny stubborn woman. "In the van now."

She shook her head.

His wolf pushed up, wanting to dominate her and teach her who was alpha in the situation. He growled, the sound low and deep. Normal people would have wet themselves just hearing it. This hardheaded female didn't even bat an eye. She did, however, jut out her chin in defiance before giving him the finger.

Giving up on trying to be nice and getting her to follow along for her own good with crazy people on the loose trying to kill folks, Roi bent, scooped her up, and tossed her over his shoulder. She smelled as sweet upside down as she did right side up.

That has its advantages, he thought to himself.

Missy hauled off and whapped him a good one in the back, and it actually hurt. He grunted but managed to keep hold of her despite how much she was wiggling.

She bit him and he roared. "Ouch!"

"Put me down, dickhead."

"I thought I was a pig's asshole," he returned, keeping her over his shoulder as he tried and failed to put her in the van.

"Argh," she snapped, hitting his back again.

Green cleared his throat from the driver's seat. "If you could speed this along."

"You try getting her in here."

"Nope," said Green with a wink. "That is all you, my friend."

The entire reason Missy and Melanie were even with them was because Green had radioed them inside the bar, informing him that the redheaded female had been injured and they needed to move out fast. Roi had been the one to make the choice to bring the other two girls back with them. Part of his decision was based on pure selfishness. He wanted to fuck Missy. Her tight ass called to him on a primal level. He wanted to have it wrapped around his cock and soon. The other reason for his decision to bring the girls was out of fear that whoever Lukian had encountered in the woods would come after the girls if left unattended. No, he didn't want anything happening to the feisty one over his shoulder.

She bit him again, and he wondered if he should change his mind. His cock twitched once more. Nope. She was what he wanted all right.

"Listen," said Lance delicately, from inside the van. "Your friend is in some real danger here, ladies. We're trying to help."

"Is she okay?" asked Melanie.

"We don't know," supplied Lance. "The sooner we get to her, the better."

"Peren needs me!" yelled Missy. "Put me

down."

"No."

The harder she kicked at him and dug her nails in his back, the more Roi wanted to take her to his bed and punish her. He'd never had a woman respond to his advances with hostility before. This was uncharted territory for him and he liked that.

She'll come around.

He tossed her in the van and climbed in beside her. Her short dress rode up and over her hips, showing off a hot little pair of pink panties. He let a bit of the wolf up and sniffed to see if he'd made her wet and was shocked to find he hadn't. He was a good-looking man and he knew it. Women usually threw themselves at him. This little one didn't seem interested in him in the least. His lips curved into a smile when she sat up abruptly and smacked his face for sneaking a peek at her undies.

Yes, ma'am, make me mind.

"You are *so* a pig's asshole!"

Yep, I am, and you, my sexy little hellcat, are

going to the safe house with us. Like it or not.

Chapter Seventeen

Peren's eyes opened, and she found herself staring into a pair of royal-blue eyes as she lay in an unfamiliar room. She blinked twice, thinking it a dream. Then the events in the woods hit her hard. Her body reacted to the fear and she tried to get up. Her legs quivered, and her stomach twisted into a knot. Suddenly feeling faint, she needed some air.

A warm hand stroked her forehead softly. "No, baby, don't move. Just rest."

"Luke?"

He smiled down at her. Why was he calling her baby? And why did it make her insides want to turn to goo? Why was she dreaming about stroking his cock? She didn't know, and she didn't care. She moved her hand up and touched his black curls. A tear rolled down her cheek, but she knew it wasn't her own. It was Lukian's pain she felt. His sadness had manifested itself in her, causing her to weep for him.

This had happened to her on several

occasions in her life. It scared her. She pulled her hand away and felt his overwhelming need to kiss her.

She tipped her head upward to meet his. Warm lips came down on hers, almost crushing her at first. Her dream flooded back to her and the panic in her rose again. Lukian got control of himself and pushed his tongue gently into her mouth. Heat washed over her, causing her nipples to harden and her body to perspire.

What's happening to me?

His tongue dove around in her mouth, exploring her, charting areas she hadn't even known existed. She pushed at his tongue with hers, panting softly, feeling the weight of his body moving over hers. Lukian cupped her face in his large palm and she planted tiny kisses on it, noticing how rough it was. He fanned his fingers out and caressed her face. Peren drew his middle finger into her mouth and sucked softly on it. He pulled it out slowly, but she hurriedly latched on to it again.

Lukian's eyes closed and his mouth

opened. She knew an invitation when she saw one and she wanted to accept it far more than she should. She wanted him above her, driving in and out of her. She didn't want to bother with foreplay or anything else that might hinder him ramming into her.

She wanted to be fucked by him, so hard and long that she'd forget about monsters chasing her in the woods, forget about Kyle going missing, and forget her own name if need be.

Chapter Eighteen

A low trickle of laughter surfaced in Lukian when Peren's thoughts rushed over him. She wanted to be taken by him and pounded until she was in a state of oblivion. That was exactly what he wanted to do to her. He wanted to take her luscious body, fuck it, mark it, and claim it as his.

Lukian looked down into her green eyes and wondered how the lover she still longed for could have left her. Her beauty alone was enough to hold any man close to her, and he knew that wasn't all there was to her. No, Peren Matthews was a complicated young woman. That much he was sure of.

He was also sure she'd change her mind on wanting to be fucked by him. While he wanted it too, he didn't want to take advantage of her fragile state of mind. Damn, it sucked being an honorable gentleman sometimes.

He hated to leave her side, but he wanted to triple-check the security around the safe house. He knew he was anal about it, but the woman he wanted to spend the rest of his life with was lying there, needing his protection, and he'd be damned if he wouldn't give it.

Spend the rest of my life with?

That phrase struck him with some force. He'd had many women in his immortally long life. He'd never once wanted to claim one as his own, as a mate. Peren made him crave that. To have her walk with him as his mate would be the greatest gift ever. He dared not wish for it, fearing that the gods would punish him for being so selfish as to think a woman as perfect as Peren would accept him, but it didn't matter, she made him want to offer her the world regardless of the potential backlash.

Reluctantly, he pulled away from her and walked toward the bedroom door. Her eyes were closed when he looked back at her. She'd had a long night. What had her friend downstairs said? Now he remembered. It was her twenty-fourth birthday. Well over a century separated them, age-wise. Thankfully, he didn't look a day over thirty. Most people had a hard time believing he was even that old. No, age wouldn't be the major barrier between them; his condition would.

He'd read her fears as she ran from him in the woods. He knew that shifters had attacked her more than once now and that one had been responsible for the death of her mother. Peren wouldn't want to be near him if she knew what he really was. Telling her seemed so unimportant next to touching her.

He walked to the room down the hall from his and tapped on the door lightly. He opened the door slowly and heard the sounds of sex. He looked in to see his field operator, Lance, pumping himself into Peren's blonde friend, Melanie. He had her bent over before him. Lance looked over at him and smiled wide as he ran his fingers down the girl's back. She was too busy holding on to the bedrails, screaming out for Lance to fuck her harder, to even notice Lukian standing there.

Lukian concentrated on Lance's thrusts, not out of the need to watch him have sex with her, but out of the need to make sure that Lance was using protection. He was. Lukian backed out of the room, nodding his head softly.

Can't risk getting a human pregnant. It could kill her.

He'd tried to instill that in his men's heads from day one. He was the only one on the team who had been born a lycan. One had survived an attack. The rest were man-made. Roi was part wolf, like him. In fact, it had been Lukian's own DNA injected into Roi. Green was part panther, as was Lance. Wilson was part rat and Jon was part tiger. They had most of the bases covered. It was an odd grouping. In nature, these animals would never run together, but in their unit it worked out well. He was the alpha male, their captain. No one questioned him. He'd never really given them a reason to until Peren.

His team had been brought in to eliminate her. They answered to the highest men in the military and no one else, but he wasn't foolish enough to think that the orders came from there. No, someone with a shitload of money had wanted Peren out of the picture and almost had their way tonight. Almost.

Lukian walked down the stairs quietly and listened as Roi and the other girl, Missy, argued in the kitchen. She still wanted to go home and Roi was still trying to convince her that it was too dangerous. Lukian stopped and laughed when he heard Missy call Roi a pig's asshole—again. Yep, Roi had finally met his match.

He continued down the hall to the basement door. He was pleased with himself for setting up nearly twelve of these types of safe houses around the states. He'd managed to set up more than fifty in foreign countries over the past twenty years. It was always easier to do bizarre things in other countries. Americans, post 9/11, had become more vigilant. Everyone was suspicious of everyone now.

He pushed the door open and headed down to Green's lab. He turned the corner and found the redheaded man busy at work. Green had his eyes pressed firmly to his microscope as he babbled to himself.

"Interesting."

"What's interesting?" Lukian asked.

Green spun around and shook his head. "Try not to do that. You nearly gave me a heart attack."

"Sorry. What's interesting?" He smiled softly. Green had survived an attack by a werepanther decades ago but had never taken to the predator side of the beast. He was easy to sneak up on when he was preoccupied.

Green pulled up a picture on his computer screen and pointed to it. "Look here, the target's...Peren's," he corrected himself quickly. "Her DNA is a melting pot. Look," he said, pulling up another page. "This is normal human DNA. This here is normal shifter DNA, and here's hers. Notice the extra strings? She's not human, Lukian, and she's not *just a shifter* either, she's..." He seemed to be searching for the best way to tell him this.

"She's what?"

"She seems to be a living and breathing incubator for various strains of supernatural creatures. There are signs of vampire, human,

Fae, and shifter blood in her. I'm also picking up bits and pieces of cells that I can't yet identify. I do know that the wolf blood is prominent, I think because of the attack you told me about. She showed me the scars on her leg. Pretty nasty. She's lucky she didn't lose her leg. I'm guessing that having vampire and Fae DNA in her sped up the healing process. That would also account for her throwing out that jolt of energy you felt when she first touched you." He took a deep breath. "There's something else."

"Go ahead," he said grudgingly.

"Her father is Dr. Lakeland Matthews. One of the scientists brought in to help stabilize the Ops program. Someone who would have had access to the experiments and DNA samples."

Lukian's stomach dropped. "Oh God. He was a major contributor to the program until he suddenly went cold turkey," he thought back, "almost twenty-five years ago." His mouth was suddenly very dry. "Green, you don't think he did this to his own daughter, do you?"

"No. Well, I wouldn't think so. It's impossible to do this to someone and not kill them or leave them as a vegetable for the rest of their life. I can't explain what she is or how she came to be it. I think this happened because of his involvement with the creation of the Immortal Ops, but I don't think he did it on purpose. At least, I hope that he didn't do it on purpose."

Chapter Nineteen

Peren sat on the edge of the large bed and pulled up her feet. She was thankful for the t-shirt and sweatpants Lukian had given her to change into after her shower. Being attacked in the woods, and then, upon her arrival at the safe house, subjected to endless tests from his friend, Green, left her feeling tired and on edge. Green had tried to be quick, but he was the stereotypical man of science, wanting to perform every test possible on her. She knew his kind. Her father was one and Kyle had been another. She was actually surprised she'd managed to get out of the testing when she did and that it wasn't still going.

She had wanted to let her father know that she was okay, but Lukian had thought it was best that she and her friends just lie low for a while. After spending some time watching Lukian and the men he called friends, it didn't take her long to figure out they were some sort of paramilitary group. She'd grown up around enough talk of government covert operations to make her immune to it—almost.

A cool brush of energy prickled over her, and she knew Lukian was headed back up the stairs to her room. She turned to the door and watched it open slowly. He poked his head in quietly, obviously expecting to find her asleep.

His blue eyes narrowed as he saw her sitting up. "You should be resting."

"I feel fine. I'm a fast healer. Always have been."

"You have no idea," he said so quietly she almost missed it.

She turned her head away from him. Staring at his muscular arms and wide shoulders made her mind wander to thoughts of sex with him. Why didn't her hormones understand she was in crisis mode? Now wasn't the time to be lusting after the hunk who had saved her life. Her hormones didn't give a crap. They wanted the man—beast-men stalking her and missing boyfriends be damned.

Stupid hormones.

Lukian stepped closer to her and her gaze

traveled the length of his body. The man looked like he could bench-press a small country. It was easy to imagine him using that same powerful frame to brace himself above her as he drove himself in and out of her. Heat flamed her upper chest and cheeks as she got a pretty good mental picture of that very thing happening. Her hormones applauded.

Their gazes locked. For a second, she thought for sure she could see his soul and it was a perfect match for her own. This was all happening so suddenly. Too fast for her to be able to catch her breath, let alone think clearly. It was all she could do to remain on the bed and not throw herself at the man. This wasn't like her. Not at all.

It had taken her almost a year to find Kyle remotely sexy. His looks weren't the problem. Most girls on campus drooled over him. The Science Department had had a boom in class registration when he'd come on to instruct some courses. She'd gone through high school and the greater part of college and remained a virgin. She'd dated a number of men, but never found one sexually appealing. A year after her father first introduced her to his new hire, Kyle, she suddenly found him so irresistible that at times she could scarcely keep her hands off him. It was as if someone had flipped a switch in her. A switch they were currently jumping up and down on when it came to Lukian.

Now she sat on the bed, forcing her hands under her legs to keep from reaching for Lukian. Something about him called to her and made her want to run her fingers through his dark black curls, and to see what hidden wonders lay under his pants and t-shirt.

The bed dipped down a little and she looked to find Lukian sitting near her. He didn't try to touch her, and she was grateful. If he did, she wasn't sure she could stop herself from tearing his clothes off. He let out a tiny laugh and she glanced over at him.

"What, my not being able to sleep funny to you?"

His lips curved upward, but he kept his eyes down. "No, sorry, just, umm, nothing, sorry."

She rolled her eyes and turned to lie back down on the bed. Lukian went to get up to give her room for her legs. *Don't go. Please, don't let him go. I feel safe with him near me. I can sleep when he's close.*

Lukian sat back down at the foot of the bed. Peren didn't care what made him change his mind. She was just happy he did. Now, maybe if she was lucky, he'd lie next to her and hold her in his arms. She had no clue how to ask him to do that without looking weak, and she already felt weak enough as it was, so she just lay still and pretended to drift off.

He slid up the bed, like a cat, and moved next to her. He swept her long hair out of the way and put his solid body against hers, spooning her.

Chapter Twenty

Lukian lay there, listening to Peren's breathing as she drifted off to sleep. He could barely contain his excitement enough to lie still and hold her in his arms. She'd wanted him to stay with her. He made her feel safe, and that was what he wanted most. Being a gentleman was hard. But every now and then he'd let his fingertips brush the underside of her breast while she slept. Sure, that was hardly behaving himself, but it was better than what he wanted to do—roll over onto her and fuck her brains out.

"Luke," she cooed in her sleep.

The sound of his name falling from her sweet lips made him even harder. He knew he couldn't walk with as hard as his cock was, so running away wasn't an option. If this kept up much longer, he'd be screaming in want for her and possibly shape-shifting. He'd never felt this raw need to be with someone before, and it actually left him a little scared. Fear wasn't something he felt often.

Peren moved in her sleep and called out his name again. She turned slightly, leaving her large breast firmly and fully in his hand. His finger ran over her soft nipple and found it responding to his touch. Everything in his brain said to get up and leave her alone. She was just an innocent, scared young woman who was reaching out to someone she believed could protect her. Even as he thought it, he knew that it wasn't true. She was his mate. He was sure of it. He just wasn't sure how or why.

She's mine.

Peren moved again, running her hand over his hip. She kneaded at the material of his pants, and her nails scraped his leg. He pulled on her body and brought them even closer together. He pressed himself firmly against her back, rubbing against her. Dry humping her wasn't nearly as good as getting to be in her, but it was all he had at the moment. She reached back, her hand going to his groin. He sucked in his breath and was afraid to move when she grabbed hold of his cock.

Don't move, don't make a sound, maybe you

won't wake her...don't — oh!

She began to stroke him through his pants. He tried to pull her hand from him, but she wasn't having anything to do with it. She was a hell of a lot stronger than she should be.

"Peren," he whispered softly. "Baby, wake up. I can't believe I'm going to say this, but can you let go of my cock?"

She gripped him harder, nearly making him come. With a groan, he moved his head back and tried to steady his breathing. It didn't help much. The woman was going to kill him with sheer need.

"P-Peren," he managed, his hips wanting to thrust, but he succeeded in refraining— barely.

Lukian had to use more force than he wanted to loosen her hold on his cock. In all his years he couldn't remember a time when he'd turned down the offer of sex, but he didn't want her like this. He wanted her to know what was happening when he claimed her, and he most certainly would claim her.

Successful in freeing his dick from her

grasp, Lukian made a move to roll off the bed. Distance was the only answer to his current problem. Well, that and a cold shower.

"No, don't go…stay with me."

He blinked down at her, stunned to see her green gaze fixed on him.

Lukian cupped his throbbing erection. "You're awake?"

With a nod, she bit her lower lip, need reflecting in her gaze. She made a soft, almost purr-like noise that sent his wolf over the edge. Unable to stop himself, Lukian moved back onto the bed, assuming the same position he'd been in behind her. He brought his lips down on her neck and drew in her vanilla-scented skin. She wore her attraction to him like a second perfume, but she also smelled of fear. His body reacted and he wrapped her protectively in his arms.

"My sweet Peren. This is too soon."

"Like hell it is," said Peren. Her hand moved over the length of his cock and his breath hitched. She was the one who pushed down the front of his pants and cupped him before stroking him. She was the one who made the first move.

Some alpha I am.

The wolf didn't react. It didn't push at him, wanting to force her. Instead, it seemed to understand her fragile state of mind and that she required tenderness and love. Things the wolf knew the man was capable of giving. He kissed her shoulder gently, his teeth burning with the need to change and claim her, but not so much so that he couldn't hold it off for a bit. He silently thanked his wolf and then slid his hands down her back, massaging her sore muscles. Each time he rubbed he could smell the scent of her arousal increasing.

She reached behind and tried to grab him again. He caught her wrist, controlling what was happening between them. "No. Let me tend to you."

She huffed.

He smiled and moved her head forward into the pillow to allow him access to her neck. He worked out the knots that had built up there. Peren surprised him by pulling her shirt up and pushed the already loose waistband of the borrowed sweatpants down her hips. Lukian gasped before continuing onward. The feel of her smooth, soft skin only served to make him hornier—as if that were even possible.

Bending, he planted tiny kisses on her hot back, his hands trailing lower down her spine. He eased his hands up and under the remainder of her shirt and aided in easing it up and over her head. She wiggled out of it and he let it drop to the floor.

She turned with her arm cupping her exposed breasts. Lukian couldn't stop the growl that burst free from him. His wolf didn't want to wait anymore. Neither did he. He leaned forward and put his hand out. He had to touch her tight stomach. He had to run his fingers over her skin.

Peren's arm slid lower, and he was left with his face hovering over her pink nipples. His beast tried to come up while he took in her scent again. He pushed the wolf down and leaned forward, drawing her nipple into his mouth. Her body reacted as if she was cold and her nipple hardened. He pulled on it gently with his teeth, rolling it around his mouth.

He felt her desire to hold him, to run her fingers through his hair. He noticed that she was keeping her hands up above her head and knew she was afraid of the way she felt for him. He released her nipple and watched it stand at attention in the cool air of the room. The impulse to let his tongue flicker back over it overcame him and he did.

Lukian sat up and pulled his shirt off slowly.

He looks like he's been carved from marble.

Her thoughts washed over him, making him smile. He was happy she liked the look of him. It made mating easier. He tipped down and took her hand, putting his chest in her face in the process. To his surprise and delight, she bit at his skin but pulled back quickly.

Oh shit, I bit him.

It took everything he had not to laugh at her. She was so sweet and innocent, yet none of the above. He slid his hands over hers and cupped them. He could sense her desire for him to make love to her like it was his own. He could easily see himself obliging. He eased up and over her, careful to avoid crushing her with his weight.

Their lips met, and he had to focus on remaining calm out of fear of shifting forms and possibly hurting her. He wanted her so much that he didn't trust himself.

Peren broke the kiss and put her lips to his neck. He knew then that she was fighting the inner need to mark him as well. That she felt the natural pull between them—as a mate should.

Reaching behind her head, he cupped it gently, guiding her to his neck, knowing she needed encouragement. It didn't take her long. She bit him, sending his wolf into overdrive and his cock into a state of longing. She'd done her part. She'd marked and bitten him— putting her claim on him.

The rest was up to him, but he needed a moment to temper his beast. He didn't want

Peren hurt during the mating ritual. He sat up, his intent to simply breathe deep for a moment and control his wolf.

Peren used the break to wiggle out from under him and discard her sweatpants. She was left naked on the bed next to him. He knew his eyes were swirling with color as his wolf surfaced quickly. So much for trying to control his other half.

With a growl, Lukian caught Peren by the waist and deposited her on the bed before him. He spread her legs and moved between them, soaking in the sight of his woman naked. She was breathtaking.

He leaned and put his face above her pussy. Inhaling deep, he savored her sweet smell before sliding his tongue out and over her slit. She tried to squirm away, her hips bucking at him as her fingers moved into his hair, pulling his head closer to her body. He added a finger to the mix, pushing it into her wet opening and nearly coming at the feel of how tight she was. He also realized he'd never fit in her without preparing her more. He added a second finger, patiently allowing her cunt to adjust to the size of the intrusion.

Lukian pushed a third finger in to spread her more. He didn't want to cause her pain but wanted to stretch her body to be sure she'd accept all of him. He licked along the inner ridge of her pursed lips, finding her clit, red, swollen, and waiting for him. He slid his mouth over it and drew it in gently. In a flash, he was running his tongue over it quickly, then stopping to suck on it. He kept his fingers moving in and out of her, leaving the fruits of his labor dripping down his hand and over her sweet ass. He brought his tongue down to lap it up. He didn't want to let a good thing go to waste.

He let one of his fingers slide into her tight ass, pushing past the pink rosette. She cried out and bucked against his hand, riding his fingers harder. Lukian pushed his face deep into her hot little cunt, licking her, fucking her with his fingers.

No…more…more…oh, Luke…oh.

He laughed softly into her as he heard her

thoughts projected onto him. He pulled his face away from her very swollen, very wet pussy and slid his pants off.

"Please," she whispered. "More."

He flicked his tongue over her clit and shoved his fingers in deep, his body responding as her pussy clamped down around him. Peren cried out as her orgasm struck, making Lukian swell with pride and need.

Chapter Twenty-One

"Please," Peren repeated, knowing she sounded pathetic begging the man, but she wanted more. She leaned up on her elbows and found Lukian standing at the foot of the bed, stroking his hard cock. He leaned forward and stuck his finger deep within her and pulled it out, taking with it a string of her come.

She bit her lip and drew in her breath as she watched him rubbing her come on his shaft until it glistened. She pulled her legs up and out, showing him that she was ready and willing to accept him, if she could. Her eyes widened as he seemed to grow larger by the second. His length was impressive, but that wasn't what made her doubt if she could handle him. It was his girth. She'd never dreamt they came in that size.

How the hell does he walk and not fall forward from the strain of that?

She watched as a tiny smirk came over Lukian's face. He climbed onto the bed on all fours and crawled over her. The primal look on his face said that he was thinking only of sticking his cock deep within her. She should have been ashamed of herself for falling into Lukian's bed so fast, but instead she regretted having not met him sooner. She wanted him deep within her, like she'd never wanted anything in her life before. The need for air seemed secondary next to the need to have Lukian's cock between her legs.

She put her hands around his neck, trying to pull his head down to her, but he stayed suspended above her. She clung to his body like a rag doll, wanting him to slam into her and grind her into a state of numbness. The tip of his cock touched her entrance. His shoulders tightened…he was about to pull away.

"No," she pleaded as she tugged on his neck. She wouldn't let him back out now. Every fiber of her being wanted him and she'd have him.

The look in his unnaturally blue eyes said that he was doing everything in his power to restrain himself. She kissed along his jawline and tried to coax him into her. He didn't budge.

He's going to stop this. He doesn't want me.

"I want you more than life itself, Peren," he said softly to her.

"Then take me," she panted.

She looked at him and willed him to have her, to use her, to make her his own. Something about this glorious man called to her on a primitive level. She wrapped her legs tight around his waist and let her upper body drop to the bed. She used her many years of training for purely selfish gain and flipped Luke over onto his back.

She pushed herself down onto him in one fluid motion, taking his shaft deep into her. She was so tight, and he so large, that she thought he might rip her in two. She cried out, as did he. He tore into her, filling her with a mix of pleasure and pain. She leaned down onto him and found his mouth. His tongue met hers and his hands went to her waist. She matched the tiny swirl-like motion that she was making with her tongue with her hips.

"Peren, you feel so damn good," he said, with a low growl.

His scent, a cross between sweat and musk, sent her pheromones into overdrive. She thrust herself onto him, taking him deeper within her. The pressure was so great that she had to pull away from his mouth to let the cries within her out. The cool air from the room made its way between them, and she took a deep breath in, trying to avoid hyperventilating. His hands moved to her hips and yanked her body down onto his, harder and faster. She had to use her arms to steady herself, moving up and down on him.

"Oh yes, Lukian, yes!"

Chapter Twenty-Two

Being sheathed inside Peren's body left him feeling removed from himself. She was so hot and tight that he felt as if he was dipping himself into a vat of hot oil. She was teasing him, her ample breasts bouncing in his face. He leaned up and grabbed hold of a nipple, sucking hard. Peren's rhythm changed. She slammed down on him so fast and furious that their bodies began to make slapping noises. Sweat-soaked and past the point of being able to stop, he tried to lift her off him. He gave one final suck of her erect nipple and looked up into her face.

"Off…off…I'm gonna…come," he said frantically.

Her eyes shifted colors, like his could do if he wasn't careful. The green in them deepened and the tiniest hint of amber wolf pushed through. She leaned down and grabbed his head to her chest. Her warm breasts pushed into his face. He fought the urge to bite down on them and leave his mark. He wanted to claim her as his own, but…

"Off…baby, I can't hold it…I'm going to come in your hot, wet…oh…" His voice sounded weak, even to him.

She yanked the hair on the back of his head and slammed her body onto him. She tightened around him as her orgasm hit, contracting, milking him. Her eyes rolled back slightly.

Give it to me…I want to feel your hot come in me…I want to feel you exploding deep inside me… "Luke…" she said softly.

Unable to hold it any longer, he released his seed into her. It erupted with such force that he shook. He grabbed Peren and pulled her to him, his cock still deep within her. He sank his teeth into her tender flesh and savored the coppery taste of her blood before licking the wound and watching it heal over instantly. It felt as if tiny, invisible threads were pushing in and out of them, weaving them together as one.

"You're mine now…forever," he stated, very matter-of-factly.

"I know," she said, rolling to the side, falling next to him on the bed.

He pulled her into his arms and kissed her forehead. She moaned slightly and moved her leg over his. The smell of her sex filled the room. He should have been sated, full, satisfied. Instead, he was left wanting even more of her. "Peren, baby."

"Hmm?" she asked lazily.

Lukian stroked her auburn hair and kissed her again. "Take me in your mouth. I want to feel those soft lips wrapped around me."

She lay still for a moment and he thought she'd say no. When her tiny hand wrapped around his still-hard cock, he knew she'd do as he asked. She slid down the bed and planted tiny kisses on his abs as she went. She reached the base of his penis and giggled slightly.

His brow creased as he leaned up to look at her. "What? Laughing at a guy in that position could cause him lasting damage."

"No, Luke, I didn't mean to laugh. I'm nervous. I've never done this before," she said, slightly embarrassed, her cheeks reddening.

"Oh baby, talk like that will get you flipped over and that sweet little ass of yours attacked. I can't control myself when I'm near you. I want you, all of you."

He reached into her hair and coaxed her mouth near him. He could read her thoughts and she wanted to take him into her mouth, her ass, wherever he wanted to take her. She was his mate, no doubt about it.

Peren's tongue ran out and over him, sending shivers down his legs. She took him slowly into her hot mouth and inched her way down his shaft. The head of his cock touched the back of her throat and her eyes widened. It took her a minute to move, but when she did, it was pure ecstasy. Each lick, each suck, sent his body over the edge and the wolf closer to the surface.

He growled out and tossed his head back, letting his balls tighten, coming down her throat. She drank him down, sucking softly, not missing a drop. Lukian's legs jerked and Peren continued to move her mouth up and down on him.

He pulled on her head gently. "Baby, I'm done."

She moved her mouth off him and licked her lips. "No, you're not. You're going to fuck me again," she said in a sultry voice.

Lukian laughed, deep and long. "Oh baby, you're killing me."

Chapter Twenty-Three

Lukian lay perfectly still, holding Peren in his arms. She'd been asleep for several hours now. After making love several more times in the bed and twice in the shower, Peren was exhausted. He was grateful she hadn't seemed to regret what they'd just done. In truth, she had no idea what they'd done, he knew that. How could she? He tried to think of the various ways to tell her that he'd just claimed her as his mate, his wife. He'd never had a mate before. He'd had lovers, even a few who meant a great deal to him, but never any who made him feel the way he felt with her—complete.

He had wanted to steal away and ask Green how his research was coming. It had been careless of him to lose control and finish inside her. If it turned out that her body wasn't supernatural enough to accept his seed, then she would never end up getting pregnant, or worse yet, would get pregnant and die.

Lukian took a deep breath and buried his

face in her silky hair. He silently prayed for her to be physically able to be his mate in every sense of the word. He wasn't sure he could go on if she wouldn't be in his life, or if he'd hurt her in any way. It was bittersweet, thinking of her possibly carrying his child. He would never forgive himself if harm came to her because of it.

His mind raced to his men. He'd spent the last how many decades lecturing them on the need for safety, for control. They didn't lead normal lives. Being a member of an elite, supernatural, special operations team didn't leave much room for a family. The other men were young yet. They weren't over fifty. Except for Green. He, too, was old.

Green had been in his early thirties and a scientist when he'd volunteered for the experiment. He was one of only a handful of survivors. The only reason he'd made it through was that he'd been attacked by one of the captive weres and not injected with serum. He came by his panther part honestly; there was nothing man-made about him. The dawning of the madman in Germany put an end to America's secret experiments for close to twenty years after that. They in no way wanted to be associated with the likes of that maniac.

None of the other men looked a day over twenty-five, the age they'd been when they joined the program. In the scope of immortals, they were babies. They most likely wouldn't feel the need to reproduce for another twenty years or so. He, on the other hand, was much older than fifty and had believed he would never find his mate.

Now, as he lay with Peren in his arms, he suddenly felt unsure. Not of her or what they'd done, but of what to do next. According to the code of the shifters and supernaturals, Peren was now considered their leader as well. She was his chosen mate and most likely the future mother of his children. Her word carried as much weight as his, in theory. He knew that it would be a difficult sell to the shifter community, especially his pack. They would naturally question his choice in a mate because she was not a full lycan. She was something, that much he was sure of, just not full werewolf. The biggest problem of all was that he knew damn well Peren had no clue what she was, or what *he* was for that matter.

He shook his head to clear his thoughts. Right now, his concern had to be about Peren's safety. Someone had paid big money to bring them in to take her down. The very thought of having even considered killing her made him flushed and nauseous. He would die before he saw her hurt, and he was guessing that would be a very real possibility when word got back to the powers that be that his team protected her.

"I'll never let anyone hurt you, my love, my wife," he whispered softly into her hair.

Chapter Twenty-Four

"You did what?" Missy demanded, in anything but a low tone. At the volume she was shouting, everyone in the safe house would hear. Instantly, Peren regretted having confided in Missy about having sex with Lukian. Wisely, she'd left out a lot of details.

Peren grabbed her friend's arm and pulled her into the tiny side room, hoping to silence her in the process. Missy had always had something of a temper. Recent events had only exaggerated it.

"Hey, announce it to the world, why don't you," Peren said in a hushed tone, though at this point she doubted it mattered how quietly she spoke.

A look of indignation came over Missy. "You fucked some ninja-Rambo-stranger? The guy's a nut. All these guys are nuts. And one of them is a pig's asshole. Peren, what if you're pregnant?"

"A pig's what?" questioned Peren, unable to follow Missy's rant with anything close to ease. She'd seen Missy lose her cool on more than one occasion in all their years of friendship. Missy tended to shout first and calm herself later. At least when it came to her friends and anything she felt put them in jeopardy.

A soft knock on the door interrupted them. Now wasn't the time to deal with anyone else. With slow, measured movements, Peren reached out and took hold of the handle. She opened the door hesitantly, worried it was Lukian and then she'd have to deal with Missy yelling at the man she thought was a ninja-Rambo-stranger, not just yelling about him. That wasn't an argument she was in the mood to have.

Seeing it was only Melanie, Peren exhaled, some of the tension in her shoulders slipping away. Dark circles had formed under Melanie's normally vivid blue eyes. Her long blonde hair, which usually never seemed out of place, was going in all directions, as if Melanie had not even bothered running her fingers through it, let alone one of the brushes Lukian had supplied all the women. Melanie pushed past Peren sluggishly and moved over to sit on one of the chairs at a long rectangular table that made Peren wonder if meetings were held in the room.

"Mel, guess what our little buddy did," said Missy, a hand on her hip and a sarcastic look on her face. "Or rather who."

Melanie's gaze met Peren's, though Melanie's eyes seemed vacant. "What did you do?" Her tone lacked any real interest.

Something was amiss.

Evidently, Missy sensed a problem as well. She stopped pushing to tattle on Peren and instead shot a look of concern in Peren's direction.

"Mel?" asked Missy, her voice barely there as she eased closer to their friend and touched Melanie's arm.

Melanie turned her focus back to Missy. A sinking feeling started in the bottom of Peren's gut. She knew without asking that something bad had happened; she just wasn't sure what it was. She pulled out one of the chairs and sat next to her friend.

"What's wrong, honey?" she asked, placing a hand upon Melanie's thigh.

Melanie turned a set of glassy eyes on Peren and spoke slowly. "I...I had sex with Lance last night."

"Something must be in the water," Missy grumbled, and Peren shot her a nasty look.

"He was just… I mean, well, he wasn't… Oh shit, he was hot and I wanted him." Melanie focused on Peren. "I got him. I got *more* than just him. We fucked three times before *it* happened."

Peren and Missy shared a perplexed expression before they inched in closer to their friend. It was Peren who spoke first. "When what happened?"

Melanie stared at the floor, refusing to make eye contact with anyone. "You won't believe me if I tell you."

"No, sweetie, it's okay. We'll believe you, go ahead," Peren coaxed, stopping only for a minute because she suddenly felt the heavy weight of someone's gaze on her. She glanced around the large meeting room but saw nothing out of the ordinary. No one was with them.

Melanie took Peren's hand and squeezed it tight. "You're going to think I'm crazy, but I swear to you...Lance changed during his orgasm."

"Changed?" Peren questioned.

Missy leaned back in her seat, a look of righteous indignation on her face. "Yeah, psycho-paramilitary freaks tend to do that. I bet he flipped out on her. I told you these guys were bad news."

Peren gave her another nasty look and pulled Melanie closer to her. "He changed how?"

"His mouth widened and then his shoulders moved up. Hair, dark black hair, sort of appeared all over him and the worst part was his teeth—they were huge. He looked like —" She gasped. "Like he was going to tear me apart after he fucked me and eat me. Like an animal would. Not like a person."

"Oh, this is ridiculous," Missy said,

standing up so fast that her chair tipped over. Something in her voice was off as if she wasn't as shocked and appalled as she was pretending to be. "He obviously slipped something in your drink at the club and you were hallucinating."

Melanie wiped the tears from her cheeks. "Hallucinating? Yes, maybe, but it felt...it felt so real."

Missy waved her hand in the air, dismissing the idea. "Well, you don't have a mark on you, and since you're sitting here telling us this, he couldn't have eaten you."

Melanie nodded. "Yes, you're right. When I got up this morning, he was lying next to me in the bed, normal. I...yes, it must have been something in my drink."

Peren felt the penetrating gaze again and then smelled the faint scent of musk. *Lukian.* She felt like he was standing in the room with her, next to her, all around her. She closed her eyes for a minute and could have sworn she felt someone moving within her thoughts—as if they were no longer her own or private. As quickly as the feeling came, it left. She turned her attention back on her friend and patted her leg.

"Yes, you were tired and had too much to drink. Lance didn't slip you a thing. You were half in the bag when we got to the club and you've been running on empty with finals lately. I'm guessing the stress of all that, combined with alcohol, left you a little off." She hoped her lie would soothe her friend.

Chapter Twenty-Five

"You changed during sex?" Roi rounded on Lance.

Lukian could sense Roi's rage. Hell, Lukian even agreed with it, but he couldn't let him kill Lance.

"Calm down," he said sternly.

The room stopped buzzing with an overabundance of testosterone, and all eyes turned to him. He was their captain, their leader, and he was expected to fix this.

Wilson took a step forward and tipped his head. "Sir, maybe it would be best if we just eliminate the women. They know too much and—"

Lukian went to strike him, but Roi beat him to it, hitting Wilson first, followed closely by Lance and then Green hitting the man as well. He could understand Lance's concern. He'd smelled Lance's desire for the blonde one the minute he'd laid eyes on her. Roi was a different story. The self-proclaimed playboy rarely thought of women as anything more than objects. He'd been surprised to find Roi sleeping on the hallway floor outside Missy's locked room when he woke. Roi had been mumbling in his sleep, something about being a pig's asshole.

Lukian still wasn't sure what that had been about. All he knew was they had another problem. Lance had clearly lost control and shifted after Lukian had glimpsed him having sex with the blonde. And the blonde had seen the whole thing.

Shit.

Green pulled Roi off Wilson and turned his attention back to Lukian. "Perhaps full disclosure? It would ease their suspicions, and if they understand the stakes, they may choose the lesser of two evils."

"Captain, if I may. Wilson might have a point. I don't want to hurt 'em. They're sweet girls, but to risk the secrecy of the team? Of supernaturals?" Jon said softly from the other side of the room, his Southern accent showing through.

Lukian spun and glared at him, his nostrils

flaring, his wolf wanting to be free to slaughter the man for even suggesting such a thing. "No one will be hurting *any* of the women. Is that understood?"

"But the red-haired one…Jen or something? She was our target. We should at least hand her over to Colonel Brooks. Maybe he could figure out what to do with the other two," Wilson said, wiping his bloodied mouth. "I'm not saying it's a great idea, but it is an idea."

"Her name is Peren, and she's my mate!" Lukian roared.

Every gaze in the room landed on him. The silence was deafening. It was Roi who stepped forward first. "Brother, tell me that you didn't mate with her. Tell me that you didn't offer her your seed and bite her."

Lukian stood silently as he stared through the two-way mirror separating his team from Peren and her friends. She was still holding her friend to her, trying to comfort her. He knew she'd sensed him reading her, scanning her thoughts, and that was another sign that she was his true mate. Not that he needed any more signs. The writing was not only on the wall, the deed was done.

She was now marked and claimed.

His mind flashed back to his moment of release in her—when he filled her body with everything he had to offer, his teeth sinking into her tender flesh, sealing the deal that she would be his forever.

"Your silence speaks volumes, Lukian," Roi spat. "If she gets pregnant, she will die. What do you have to show for it then? How could you take a human mate? Tell him, Green. You're always lecturing us about the dangers. Tell him!"

Green stepped forward and cleared his throat. "Umm, here's the thing. I did some additional tests on Peren this morning. She's less human than we are."

Roi and Lukian turned to Green.

He continued, "I told you about the vampire DNA in her and what I thought might be Fae...and well, you told me about her surviving a shifter attack when she was younger. So it's obvious she carries a bit of shifter in her as well, but…"

Green glanced at Lukian, looking scared that his commander and friend would kill the messenger. Lukian nodded to him, wanting more than anything to hear what he had to say.

"Peren shows signs of having every known form of shifter DNA in her blood, along with several midlevel demons. The most shocking of all is that they have all meshed together. The only conclusion I can come to is that the same genetic engineering and splicing techniques used to create the I-Ops were used here, but it was all raw—base form kind of stuff. I'm not sure, but I think she could shift into upwards of thirty creatures and more than likely has the same powers as most vampires. She, of course, is unaware of any of this. I could sense that during the testing."

Green had the gift for reading truths. It was typically reserved for wolves and vampires, but somehow Green developed it. If he said Peren was unaware of her condition, then it was true. No one in the team would question him. They'd come to rely too heavily on each other's strengths to start doubting them now. The question that was plaguing Lukian wasn't if Peren knew what she was, but how she came to be in the first place. Someone out there knew full well what she was and wanted to put an end to her.

But why?

Lukian stormed past his friend and went straight for a burner cell to call Brooks. He pressed the send button and waited for Brooks to answer.

"Mission is complete, Colonel," Lukian said, his voice never betraying his emotions.

There was a moment of silence on the other end. "Very well. I'll expect a full briefing in the morning."

Lukian ended the call and tossed the phone aside. Not one of his men questioned him. He didn't think they would. He looked back at the mirror to stare at the three beautiful women who had gotten themselves tangled up in a mess they couldn't possibly understand.

This isn't fully about them, he thought, his

mind still racing.

He couldn't help but think back to his time in the laboratories with Peren's father. They had worked side by side in stabilizing the creation of an elite fighting team. There had been at least three tries prior to theirs—that Lukian was aware of. He suspected there had been more he wasn't told about. All were unsuccessful. Synthetic serums had been used to try to re-create the DNA and induce change. Most of the men had died. Others had been left broken in some fashion and labeled Outcasts.

He turned and looked at the five men standing near him. Each had been carefully screened. It had been determined that all had traces of supernatural abnormalities in their blood prior to the start of the experiments. Somewhere in each man's family history there had been an event that no one talked about. Lukian had spent well over a hundred years roaming this earth and had come into contact with more immortals than he cared to count. He was able to round up enough pure blood samples for Dr. Matthews, and that had helped stop the senseless deaths. His team had known the risks before they went into the testing and they knew the consequences.

All but one from his team had survived. Roi had been selected as a backup initially. He'd been an alternate candidate. The man prior to him had been given too much of Lukian's straight blood, and the effects had been devastating. Parker, the man in question, had been unable to control the changes, lost his mind, and escaped. They'd searched for him for the last twenty-five years, but he'd managed to drop off the face of the earth. The chances of him surviving had been so minimal that continuing to spend money and man-hours in search of him was ridiculous.

Deep down Lukian began to worry that everything that had happened in the last twenty-four hours had been orchestrated to bring them to this point—and that they were merely puppets being toyed with by a master manipulator. Someone wanting to call the shots.

He hoped he was wrong.

Chapter Twenty-Six

Peren eased closer to Melanie on one of the oversized sofas in the safe house living area. Lukian had explained the home was never used and had been set up, like many, to be somewhere he and his team could go should they have the need. This apparently counted as having need. She'd not been able to get much out of Lukian on just what type of team he and his men were, but she had her suspicions. They were probably military. At least she hoped that was the case. She didn't want to allow her mind time to race on all the other possibilities. She had enough strange things happening in her life. She didn't need to add conspiracies to the mix.

Whatever they were, it must have paid well because the safe house was large and decorated with high-end furniture. The men all had clothing here as well and had managed, between the lot of them, to materialize sweatpants and t-shirts for all of the women, as well as toiletries.

The safe house felt homier than Peren's actual family home. One of the men had selected a movie for everyone to view and it was currently playing on the big-screen television. It was about people driving fast in cars. She didn't exactly get the appeal, but the men seemed to enjoy it.

Missy refused to sit. She'd been agitated from the moment they'd pulled into the safe house's driveway and hadn't let up since. Not that Peren could blame her. Everything was crazy and none of it made a lot of sense.

Missy glanced toward the clock on the wall, again, and then stared boldly at Lukian. "You said you'd give us a ride home nearly four hours ago. We'd call for a taxi but your goons have our cell phones and this place doesn't have a phone."

"They aren't goons," said Peren in a tone she hoped would defuse the situation.

"Not true," said Lance. "Roi is a goon."

"And then some," added Missy.

Lukian's gaze landed on Peren. She hadn't confessed to her friends about the wolves in

Immortal Ops

the woods outside the bar or the beast man who had dragged her by her hair and licked her before hurting her. She'd not even fully confessed everything to Lukian. Kyle had been the only one she'd ever trusted with information about men who could shift into wolves, and he was gone. She couldn't tell her friends and have them look at her as if she was crazy. They did that enough already since Kyle had vanished. No. She'd been as vague as possible about the entire ordeal, hoping they'd just trust her enough to remain at the safe house and stop asking questions.

Unfortunately, Missy was a question master. By day she was a system analyst, and apparently, in her off time she was an interrogator, because she had a never-ending supply of questions and the intimidating stare to back them up. She zeroed in on Roi, who had been sneaking peeks at her all day between making snide comments that only served to piss her off. Peren was stunned Missy hadn't beat the crap out of the guy yet. Missy narrowed her gaze on Roi. "I'm hungry."

Roi leapt to his feet and nearly tripped over Lance in the process as he made a play for the hallway. Lance caught him and steadied the guy. "Take it easy."

The man she'd heard Wilson refer to as a color came around the corner and paused, his gaze on Lance and Roi. "Tell me Roi isn't trying to kill Lance now too. It's all we can do to keep him from going after Wilson nonstop."

"That is true, Green," said Lukian with a nod.

A man who was lying sideways in a recliner, his feet draped over the edge, grinned and waved at the group. He blew on his knuckles. "That is right, folks. I'm normally the center of his pissed-off attention. Now I'm competing against Ms. Personality over there." He motioned to Missy who, in turn, flipped him off. "Case in point."

Roi moved around Lance, heading in the direction of the kitchen. He returned within seconds, looking winded and holding a menu in one hand. His gaze locked on Missy. "How about Chinese takeout in honor of Missy?"

Peren lowered her head, unable to look at the mess Roi had just talked himself into. Without looking up, Peren nodded, already knowing what was coming as she rubbed her temples. Her friend was going to go off on the man.

Missy choked out a snort. "Why would Chinese food honor me? I'm half-Vietnamese, dickhead."

Wilson cracked up, laughing so hard he squeaked, nearly falling from his chair.

A tall blond with off-putting amber eyes stepped into the room. He'd been scarce at the safe house, and the few interactions Peren had had with him, he'd been quiet and reserved. He seemed so somber and serious that Peren wasn't sure what to expect. As he raised a plastic weapon and fired directly at Wilson, leaving a bright orange suction cup dart stuck to Wilson's forehead, Peren smiled wide.

Wilson yanked the dart off and threw it at the man. "Jon, isn't that getting old?"

"Not even a little," said the man, a Southern accent showing through.

Lance high-fived Jon. "Nice. I told you it was fun. That has been the best four-dollar purchase I've ever made."

Missy looked Roi up and down, ignoring the other men's playfulness. "You're still a pig's asshole."

Roi flashed a bad-boy grin and took off for the kitchen again.

"Ten bucks says he's trying to find a menu with Vietnamese cuisine featured on it," said Wilson, shaking his head.

Lance and Jon pulled their wallets out. Lukian growled and then the men put their money away.

Lukian glanced at Missy. "My apologies for Roi."

"It's not your fault he's annoying." Missy put her hand out to Jon and motioned with her fingers for him to surrender the dart gun. He did and then armed her with darts as well.

Lance made a move to assist her with loading it, but she shook her head. "I've got it. Thanks."

Roi returned with another menu in hand.

"How about pizza?"

Missy took aim, fired, and scored a direct hit to his groin before reloading and then shooting Roi right between the eyes. Neither dart stuck, but the one between the eyes left a mark for a moment. Everyone, including Lukian, laughed.

Wilson leaned and gazed up at Missy. "If you were aiming for his brains, you got them with your first shot."

"Oh, I know," replied Missy with a wink.

Roi bent, picking up the darts with a groan. He handed them to Missy. "Are you going to kiss my boo-boos now?"

She glanced at Peren. "I might have to kill this one."

"She's a touch nicer when she's been fed," offered Peren apologetically to Roi before glancing at Lukian, who seemed more amused than anything else.

His blue gaze moved to her and she blushed, having to look away as she thought about what they'd done upstairs only hours earlier. Lukian pushed Wilson's legs off the side of the chair and then sat on the arm of the chair. He winked at Peren and she jerked closer to Melanie.

Melanie put her head against Peren's shoulder. Peren noticed that it was the big guy named Green who moved in Melanie's direction first—beating out Lance, as if he wanted to comfort her.

Peren closed her eyes a moment and silently prayed Melanie wouldn't sleep with that guy too. That was all she needed right now. Two big guys going to blows over Melanie. It had happened before and would more than likely happen again.

"Roi, order food," said Lukian, standing and drawing the attention of the men. "Ladies, if you don't mind, I'd like to go speak with my friends a second."

Missy shrugged. "Can the topic of taking us home come up in there?"

Melanie nodded. "I want to go home. Let's call my brother."

Eadan Daly would come running if he thought the girls needed help. Deep down

Peren knew that would cause more problems than it would solve. Her friends didn't know she was being hunted by things that weren't human. She didn't want to involve Eadan in it all too.

Chapter Twenty-Seven

"We need to get out of here," Missy said softly as she and Peren rinsed the dishes from dinner. The safe house was equipped with just about everything—except paper plates. Peren didn't turn to acknowledge her friend's statement, she just nodded. Missy was right, she knew that. They needed to go home. The thought of leaving Lukian made her sick to her stomach, but the thought of staying scared her just as badly. She'd spent the greater part of the day avoiding him. He'd tried to talk with her once, but she'd turned away and left him standing alone. It was the hardest thing she'd ever done.

A light pain started in her temple. She'd been experiencing the pains since Melanie had told her about Lance's change. She kept feeling like something was trying to push through her head. The only thing that helped was to imagine a wall around her, protecting her, shielding her, for lack of a better word. She'd asked Green for an aspirin, and he had been the one to suggest trying the semi-meditation techniques. They'd been working out well for her. Green seemed like a nice man. He was handsome and, as far as she could tell, unattached. She'd wished that it had been he that Melanie had fallen for, not Nordic god Lance.

She finished with the dishes and headed upstairs to check on Melanie. Voices floated to her from the other end of the hallway. Peren sank back into the corner and stood silently, needing to understand what was going on in the house.

"I can't believe that little prick even suggested hurting them. I should have ripped his fucking head off." She knew that deep voice. It was Roi, the one who stayed close to Lukian and the one Missy had taken to only referring to as Pig's Asshole.

"I know, I feel the same way," Lukian answered.

"Of course you feel the same. I still can't believe you took her as your mate. The others in the pack will be hesitant to call her their queen. Doesn't matter what she is, Lukian, she's not fully one of us. Hell, does she even know about you?"

"No," Lukian said softly. "I'm not sure how to tell her. Any suggestions on how to do it?"

"Oh, I don't know, you could try the truth. Peren, I fucked you, came in you, and cemented a bond that's eternal. Try to back out and I'll be left no choice but to carry out my original orders. How's that for a proposal? Maybe telling her she's now royalty would help. Chicks like to be called princess and queen and shit."

Lukian growled. "Stop bringing that up. I've told you already that part of my life isn't important to me."

Roi shrugged. "If I were king, I know I wouldn't shrug it off. No worries...so...what about this girl?"

Peren fought to control her breathing. What the hell were they talking about? It had to be her and Lukian, but what was all this nonsense about forever and royalty? Yeah, the thought of waking up in his arms every day made her want to do backflips, but he was involved in some heavy shit and she didn't want to get in any deeper than she already was.

"Are you going to tell her about yourself?" Roi asked.

There was a pause before she heard Lukian reply. "Again, I'm still trying to figure out how to tell her. She needs to know about her genetic makeup, as well. That should come from her father. He has to know. A man like him, with his history in genetics and his part in the Ops Program, he can't be clueless on what his daughter really is. Oh gods, what if he did that to her? What if he's why she is what she is? How do I tell her that?"

"What kind of sick bastard does that to his own daughter?" Roi asked.

"Here's the thing. I knew him, Roi, and the man was the type who'd lasso the moon for his wife. I can't see where his daughter would be any different. I remember the look on his face when he told me that his wife was expecting.

They'd been trying for years and hadn't had any luck. Dr. Matthews was on cloud nine."

Peren stood quietly, absorbing all she'd just heard. How could Lukian have known her father before she was born? He didn't look much older than her. And what was the Ops Program?

"I don't know how much her father had to do with what she is, but for now I've bought us some time with Brooks. He thinks she's dead. That'll give us some time to try to figure out who hired us to kill her."

Hired to kill me?

Peren fell back against the wall when she heard what Lukian had said. He'd been hired to kill her? She dropped back, missed the top step, slamming hard into the next one.

"What the...?" Roi said from behind her.

She turned and stared past him at Lukian. Lukian's blue eyes widened as he clearly realized she'd overheard his conversation. "Peren...shit, no!"

In an attempt to put distance between them, Peren slid down the stairs hard and fast.

The feel of the hard wood smacking against her legs made her want to stop—the thought of Lukian's betrayal kept her going. The bottom step came upon her quickly and she jumped to her feet. She turned and looked at the front door. They kept it bolted tight. They had claimed it was to keep bad things out. Now she wondered if it was really to keep her in.

She ran past the door and eyed up the front room window. Bars were on the other side. She'd noticed that earlier in the day. Her mind raced as she thought of a way out, then it hit her.

"Peren, baby…wait!" Lukian called out from behind her. His arm shot out to grab her and she ducked under him.

Roi grabbed hold of her and she brought her forehead down hard into his face.

"Son-of-a-bitch," yelled Roi as he grabbed at his nose, dropping her in the process.

She ran up the stairs, taking them three at a time. When she threw the bedroom door open, she nearly ripped it off the hinges. Footsteps followed close behind her.

*

"Shit! She's a wild one!" Roi yelled as he ran behind Lukian up the stairs.

"You've no idea!" Lukian shouted back.

Lukian ran toward the bedroom. He caught sight of Peren's hair as she ran into the room. His heart was beating so fast he thought it might leap out of his chest. He couldn't lose her, not now that he had just found her. No, she was his and he would try to make her see that he'd never hurt her.

He rushed into the room and stopped so fast that Roi ran right into him, sending both of them crashing to the ground. He looked up, alarmed, when he saw Peren diving through the window. The sound of breaking glass and cracking wood filled the air around them. He pushed to his feet, followed closely by Roi.

"Peren!" he yelled.

They were two and a half stories aboveground. Lukian hit the window and stopped, not wanting to see Peren's broken body. Roi moved past him and glanced out.

"I'll be a monkey's uncle...or wait, make that a wolf's brother, or pig's asshole, depending on who you ask." Roi's hand touched his shoulder. "It's okay, look."

Lukian turned to see Peren using a nearby tree branch to swing her body around, much the same way a gymnast would use the uneven bars. His eyes widened as she gracefully dismounted. She dropped to the ground and crouched for a moment, like a tiger. Her head turned quickly to one side. He knew that her instincts were telling her which way was home, and he knew that whoever else had been in the woods with them the other night would be waiting there for her return.

He went to leap out of the window and onto the tree. Roi grabbed his arm. "Hey, wolf boy, you're not made for swinging from trees. Take the stairs."

Chapter Twenty-Eight

Peren's bare feet pounded on the ground beneath them. Each step she took she thought about her friends and how she'd left them at the safe house with hired guns. She had to double back and get them. She had to protect them. Her mind said one thing, but her body did another. Adrenaline was pushing her, driving her onward.

When she spotted the edge of her property line, confusion hit her hard. How the hell far had she gone? How long had she been running? Her pace slowed as she ran to the iron gate. Her key card was still back at Lukian's. She rushed over to the electronic pad and keyed in the code. The darn thing didn't budge. No shock. Her father had been terrible with upkeep on nearly everything. It was all she could do to convince him to maintain one wing of the home, let alone the entire thing. They had the money. He just didn't seem to care if the place fell apart around them.

Come on, come on!

Nothing.

A rustling in the bushes caught her attention. Had the beasts from the woods near the bar tracked her again? Had they come to finish her off? She spun around to find Lukian standing there. His royal-blue gaze looked hungry as it locked firmly on her. Turning, she hit the button to the gate again. She shouted out something that wasn't even words so much as it was a cry of frustration.

Lukian grabbed her. "Peren, don't draw any more attention to yourself. You're in danger."

A wild laugh burst free from her. "Yeah, I heard all about it. What? Do you want a little more action before you bump me off?"

"Bump you off? Who even uses that phrase anymore? I've been alive a long time and I don't remember anyone other than fictitious Hollywood characters using that. I once knew a gangster, but he said…never mind." He smiled wide and continued on, loosening his grip on her as he went. "I must say that it does have a certain amount of charm when you use it. Say it again. It's adorable."

She was aghast that he was trying to make light of the situation. She'd trusted him, cared for him, and quite possibly allowed herself to fall in love with him and he'd been sent to kill her. That would end even the best of relationships.

Lukian took another step toward her and she backed up into the iron gate. She wondered if she'd have time to scale the thing before he got hold of her.

Probably not.

"Missy and Melanie?" she asked, worried about her friends' safety.

"I'm guessing Missy is still giving Roi hell and Green is probably watching over Melanie. She's pretty shaken up."

Peren thought about what Melanie had confessed to her—that Lance had changed during sex. She also thought of the conversation she'd overheard between Lukian and Roi. "What am I?"

"Not human," he said, his voice oddly even.

She didn't scream or faint, all the things that seemed expected when one received news like that. Instead, she exhaled as if she'd been waiting all her life for that confirmation. "And what about you?"

"I'm not human either."

She narrowed her gaze on him. "Honestly, I don't know that I can handle much more of the truth right now."

"Understandable."

She fought the urge to cry, feeling powerless and overwhelmed with recent events.

"Peren," he said softly, no malice to his voice. "I'm sorry you heard what you did."

"But you're not sorry you were hired to bump me off?"

His lips quirked, but he wisely refrained from laughing. "I'm sorry about that too. From the second the order was issued I had problems with it. I understand why now."

"Why then?" she demanded.

"You're not ready to hear the truth of it all," he said, easing closer.

She reached out to touch his cheek. His hand caught her wrist gently, turned her palm to his face, and kissed it tenderly. A tidal wave of heat poured through her as she stood before him. She wanted to both hit him and kiss him. It was all quite confusing.

He laughed again. "I vote for kiss me."

The second the words left his mouth she did just that, going to her tiptoes, her lips finding his. His hands found her waist as she kissed feverishly at his mouth, unable to get enough of him. It felt as if a curtain in her mind pulled back, and she recognized the strange sensation she'd been having all day. It was Lukian. *He* was in her head. He'd been invading her mind since the moment they'd met.

She thought about how he'd guessed her thoughts, about being torn between kissing him or hitting him. Mild panic swept over her as her mind raced.

He can read my thoughts

"Yes, and you will be able to read mine in time. I'm sure of it," he whispered tenderly in her ear.

"What?"

"It will come with some time, Peren."

She tried desperately to see inside his mind. Nothing but an overwhelming feeling of security came to her. He would never harm her or allow anyone else to either. Reluctantly, she drew back from him. She grabbed his hand, held it tight in hers, and turned to the gate that was now opening. The stupid thing had a mind of its own.

Chapter Twenty-Nine

Lukian wasn't sure what he'd expected the Matthews house to be, but it certainly wasn't this. The place was massive, nearly as large as his home in Maine, but not well-kept by any means. It was the mansion time had forgotten. Only the west wing was in order. The other wings had been left to their own devices.

He stared around and shook his head.

Peren took notice of him and sighed. "I don't remember a time it wasn't this way. There are a few people who come and tend the grounds and the wing where we live. They tell me that at one time the entire home was something out of a storybook. My father doesn't discuss it much."

"Peren, does he need money?" asked Lukian. "I have plenty. What is mine is yours."

She smiled at him sweetly. "That is sweet of you to offer, but we're fine. More than fine. I've sat in on meetings with my father's financial advisers. He isn't hurting for cash. He just, well, I don't know. He seems safe here but unable to let the past go. Weird, huh?"

Lukian glanced around. Yes, it was certainly strange. Lukian himself had grown up in the lap of luxury. His mother had been the only child of a wealthy family and was orphaned before she was old enough to wed. Her uncle had custody of her but was anything but civil to her. Once Lukian's father, who was rich beyond words, had appeared, the uncle had begun physically abusing her. The wolf in his father was too hard to control and the man in him would not stand by and watch the woman he loved be abused. Lukian had never been officially told how his mother's uncle had died, but he had his suspicions.

No, money had never been an issue to Lukian. He gave sizable amounts to charity each year and kept his nose clean. He lived a modest life for a man of his position and wealth, and that was perfectly fine by him. Or, at least, it had been fine with him until he stepped foot inside Peren's family home.

Lukian wouldn't allow the home to remain in this state any longer than it had to. He'd speak with Dr. Matthews, and he'd handle the repairs, even if he had to do them himself. Roi would have a field day when he found out Lukian was planning on actually spending some of his fortune. He'd been after him for years to do so. Though his friend would be disappointed it didn't involve hot triplets.

As they entered the kitchen, Peren began moving about once more, as if looking for her father. She'd been doing much the same thing since she'd led him into her home. He knew her father wasn't there, and so did she, yet she insisted on checking every room in the west wing. He needed to check in with his team, but now wasn't the time to step out and make a call. Instead, Lukian did something he and his men were capable of doing but tried to avoid because of the drain it often took on them.

He reached out with his mind, down the mental path the I-Ops used, and connected almost instantly. *I have her. She's safe.*

Good, returned Roi. *The other two are pissed. Missy has threatened to geld me if Peren doesn't show back up soon, totally unharmed.*

Lukian hid his smile. *I'm starting to like Missy more and more. She keeps you in line nicely.*

If you mean wants to put my balls in a fucking jar and then slit my throat, sure, she's great.

Lukian snorted and hid his laugh under a cough. *Whatever it takes to keep you on a leash.*

Where are you now?

Lukian glanced around. *Somewhere the Addams Family would be happy to call home. Also called Peren's home.*

That bad?

Words wouldn't do it justice. Dr. Matthews isn't here. Have Green reach out to his contacts and see if anyone has spoken to him.

Will do, Captain. Be safe.

You too.

"I don't understand," Peren said, appearing confused and breaking Lukian's mental connection to Roi. "I thought my dad would be here. We meet every Saturday morning for breakfast. He's been insistent on it since I was a child. My stepmother tried to get him to change the day, but he wouldn't hear of it. Saturday mornings were our thing. They've always been our thing."

"Stepmother?" Lukian had lost touch with Dr. Matthews shortly before Peren's birth. He didn't know he'd remarried.

Peren stared past him at nothing in particular. "I never actually knew my real mother. My father talks about me being a blessing, a miracle, but I think I'm a curse. I guess there were years of infertility and then finally, I came along. But she died during childbirth. I live with that knowledge everyday." She closed her eyes a moment. "My father remarried five years later. Susan was a wonderful mother." He could sense the dread and feeling of mourning pass over her. "She died when I was ten. She was murdered."

He fought the urge to say that he knew of the murder, that he'd picked up on her memories of it in the woods outside of the bar. She didn't need the added stress of knowing he'd been privy to vital details of her life prior to her actually sharing them with him. Besides, the information that her biological mother passed away during her birth was news to him, so he wasn't lying. He went to put his arm around her, but she continued talking. He wanted to cover her full lips with kisses and had to control himself to allow her to express her thoughts.

"Yes, Father is always on time. I generally come out here to the main house to meet him. My apartment is too small to entertain in and he loves to put on a show, even if it's just the two of us."

Her apartment?

He looked around the large kitchen and felt it then. Dread, death, despair, rage, and most of all, hate. These feelings had to be emanating from somewhere and from someone. He knew it wasn't Peren—she was too worried about her father's sudden disappearance to be projecting anything but concern. The feelings hit him stronger and he searched for the direction they were coming from—east.

"Peren, honey, what's in the other sections of the house? Are you sure no one lives there?"

Her look of bewilderment told him that no,

she didn't know that someone was there. Maybe he was just picking up on old scents and memories imprinted on the home, but something felt off.

She took hold of his hand. "There is no one here. My dad doesn't leave the main wing when he's home. And we have limited house helpers. None of them go in the other areas. I think they're scared of the older sections. Come on. I'll show you around to set your mind at ease."

Chapter Thirty

Peren followed behind Lukian as he wandered through her childhood home. He led, and she followed. It was odd at first, but he seemed like a man on a mission, so she went with it. She trailed close behind him. His musky scent blew back at her lightly as he opened the door to the east wing and she felt her knees weaken.

Why am I so drawn to you?

"Because you are my mate, my one true partner. You are mine forever, Peren," he said, looking over his shoulder at her, his blue gaze smoldering with desire.

Forever.

She let the thought of that float around. She'd believed that what she had with Kyle was special, she'd assumed that he was the one —her forever. Walking behind Lukian and looking at the way his sweat-soaked shirt clung to every ripple, wanting to tear his clothes off and let him use her any way he wanted, she knew that she'd never had this with Kyle. She touched Lukian's back lightly. He turned to her and smiled. Sex with him had been earth-shattering, but she couldn't rely on just sex the rest of her life. She needed more and believed that he would too, someday. She'd only just met the man. Forever seemed so strange to even consider with him, yet that was exactly what she wanted.

Forever.

Lukian faced her and pulled her close. "Never doubt how I feel about you again, never. Do you understand you are my mate, the only one I have ever taken? The only one I've ever given my seed to. The only woman I've ever claimed and the only one I even can claim. It is for life, Peren."

"You talk about us like we're animals," she said, half joking. Mate? Lukian had referred to her as this on more than one occasion. That wasn't a standard pet name to call your significant other.

She remembered the wolves in the woods and Lukian's lack of surprise at them. Nothing had shaken him. There were times he seemed so alpha, so incredibly in control, that he felt almost animalistic to her. Why was that? Was he like what had attacked her in the woods and also when she was ten? Was he more than simply a man? And then there was Melanie and what she said happened during sex with Lance — that he'd changed partially into an animal.

"Lance...can he...*do* anything special?" She was having a hard time coming out and saying "change into a beast."

Lukian tightened his grip on her arm. He bent his head, trying to kiss her, but she pulled away. She needed answers, not distractions. He apparently thought differently. He twisted her around and pushed her firmly against the wall before she had time to soak in what was going on. His hand went up her shirt. She gasped as he brushed over her hardened nipples.

The hard edge of his jawline held her attention. She reached out and traced the edges of his chiseled frame. His neck muscles tightened as she leaned up to plant tiny kisses on him. He pushed her hands back against the wall, effectively rendering her useless. She wanted more from him and growled in frustration, making him laugh.

"Lukian."

"I need to check something and then I'm going to do everything you want and more," he said, moving to take a step back from her. "And we can have a nice long talk then. I promise."

The strongest urge to bite him again came over her with such force that she was powerless to do anything but obey. She sank her teeth down into his shoulder blade. The bite was hard enough to get his attention, but not hard enough to draw blood. Stunned at her actions, Peren dragged her mouth off him and gasped. "Ohmygod. I'm so sorry."

She couldn't believe she'd attacked him that way—again. Lukian looked stunned but not disgusted at her behavior. The growing bulge in his pants told her exactly what he thought of her theatrics. He was turned on.

Why didn't he see her as a freak?

She saw herself as one.

He adjusted his cock through the front of his pants, groaning, his gaze going to her chest. "I want to fuck you, but now isn't the time."

"Do it. Fuck me," she said, shocking herself with her frankness. The scent of his sweat, the closeness of his body, was proving to be more than she could handle. She moved to run her fingers into the top of his pants and he grabbed her wrists gently. She pulled her hands back toward herself, bringing his with hers. If he didn't want her touching him, that was fine, she'd think of something else.

She drew his hands toward her waistband and eased it down gently. He began to pull away and then gave in to his need to touch her. His thick fingers darted quickly between her thighs and found her moist and ready for him. In a sudden fury, he was pushing against her, pinning her body to the wall. He continued his sensual assault on her silken channel, causing tiny moans to escape her throat. Each thrust left her juices soaking the both of them, running down his hand and her inner thighs.

Lukian lifted her off the ground, keeping

her pinned firmly to the wall, as he continued fingering her. She had no idea how he'd managed to get his pants down and didn't care once she felt the head of his cock pushing into her. The world around her faded away, leaving only her and Lukian. He rammed himself into her with such force that a picture fell off the wall and onto the floor. A low purring noise erupted from deep within her.

Lukian's thrusts came faster and harder. Her body struggled with something great, wild, overpowering. She tried to keep it deep within her, but her abdomen tightened and her body clenched tight around his rigid cock as he brought her to her peak. The orgasm unleashed the animal within her and she felt detached from herself as she bit down hard on Lukian's shoulder. Coppery, sweet-tasting fluid ran into her mouth. Lukian let out a growl that matched hers. She was faintly aware of a deep pressure above her right breast and of the added girth between her legs. None of that mattered. All that mattered was the pleasure washing over her. He made her feel alive. And he made her feel safe.

Chapter Thirty-One

Lukian held his mate's hand as they walked down another of the darkened halls of her childhood home. He'd planned to take her back to the safe house and discuss everything in detail with his men, but he'd gotten lost in lust and had taken Peren again. He'd never get enough of her. He knew that.

Right now he couldn't shake the sensation that they weren't alone in the giant, neglected home. The wolf in him wouldn't let him simply leave without searching the entire estate. He had to be sure. His inner alarms sounded as he caught the scent of another shifter. The hairs on the back of his neck stood on end. This was not a member of his team. He'd spent decades with these men, and he knew their scents well.

Peren stopped moving behind him. He wasn't sure if she realized it or not, but she was sensing the intruder too. If Green's findings were correct, then Peren would be more adept at tracking things than he was, once she acknowledged her powers.

He felt her reaching out to him with her thoughts. She was concerned for him and wanted him to contact the other men in his unit. He grinned, proud of his mate. She'd picked up on the fact they were a tight military unit right off the bat. Most people thought they were old college buddies. She was a smart girl who followed her instincts.

He moved down the darkened hallway, then turned and motioned for Peren to halt. He didn't want her following him into a trap. He couldn't bear the thought of one hair on her head being harmed. He loved her too much to let anything happen to her.

I love her?

As he thought more on it, he knew it was true. She was his mate. Nature made sure he loved her and he was damn thankful for that. Now that he'd claimed her, she was his, in every sense of the word. If she rejected him when she learned the truth about what he was, he'd still walk by her side, still follow close — even if in the shadows. She was his now and forever. His to love and protect. And his to watch over.

He prayed she'd accept him, because if she didn't, someone in his pack could issue a challenge to not only his rule but her as his mate. A challenge among most political decision makers meant elections or debates. A challenge among shifters meant someone died.

He would die before he allowed harm to befall her, and he'd gladly give up his throne if it meant keeping her.

"Stay put, my sweet," he said.

She nodded as he went in search of the other shifter scent he'd picked up on.

Chapter Thirty-Two

Peren hated the idea of standing around and doing nothing while Lukian went ahead without her. He didn't have to tell her that something was very wrong in the house, she felt it too. A sense of dread had fallen over the entire place shortly after they'd finished making love. The house often took on an ominous vibe, but this was more than that. It was scary now, and she'd never been scared in her childhood home before.

It'd been ten minutes since he'd vanished down the long corridor, and time felt like it was standing still. She had to take a moment to relax her breathing and focus on what was going on around her. The strongest urge to look out the window came over her, and she gave in to her gut. She moved over toward the window and stared out into the dark night. It took a moment for her eyes to adjust.

She made out two shapes near the edge of the property. They were moving with great speed along the inside of the wall. Darkness was their only cover, and Peren had no trouble seeing in the dark.

She glanced back down the hall in the direction Lukian had disappeared. If these men were trying to flank him, they would succeed if she didn't step in. Warning him felt wrong—as if yelling out might get him hurt. No. She couldn't do that. She knew she was disobeying Lukian's orders, but she'd never been much for authority. She moved against the wall and walked quietly to the first room she came to.

She opened the handle and slid quietly into the room. She moved with a stillness that caught her by surprise. The window opened with a bit of effort on her part. She climbed out slowly, covering the distance to the fence in less than a minute. That sort of speed was unheard of for humans, and she knew it. The more she thought back about her life, the less human she began to feel.

Chapter Thirty-Three

Lukian tried to lift his head. It felt as if he was smuggling bricks in it. Someone had caught him off guard and managed to get the drop on him when he'd entered the lowest level of the large home. That had never happened before, and he was curious as to how it happened at all.

Opening his eyes, he found himself staring at a dirty, bloodstained concrete floor. His wrists were chained behind his back. He tried to move his legs up and discovered his ankles were shackled as well. The more he yanked on the chains in an attempt to free himself, the more he knew they were silver-plated. Any other material he could have ripped apart easily. Silver was his weakness—as was the case for most shifters. It was one of the few things that could kill him.

His mind raced and he tried to get a bearing on where he was. His surroundings still smelled of the Matthews' estate, yet the dark cell he was in looked nothing like the rest of the house. He thought of Peren and sniffed the air, trying to catch her scent, but failing. He hoped it meant she had listened to him and stayed where he'd told her.

The odds of whoever had done this to him going after her next were great. He tried again in vain to free himself from the chains. Each attempt only made them cut deeper into his skin. If he wasn't careful, they would cut right through his body. If it meant he could save Peren, he was willing to risk life and limb.

Peren, get out of the house! Get to the safe house! Get to my men! Go. It's not safe here!

He tried to reach Peren with his mind. He had told her that she could hear him in time. He prayed that she was ready for that.

*

Peren stifled a giggle as she stared down at Roi lying on the ground. She hadn't meant to be as aggressive as she'd been, but then again, she hadn't realized it was him when she'd leapt out of the tree to try to bravely protect

Lukian. Jon, who was with Roi and who had been the second figure she'd seen from the house, hadn't stopped laughing yet. He pointed at Roi and laughed more, no sound coming out.

Roi glared up at him and growled. Jon stopped laughing and put his hand out to Roi, helping him up in the process. Roi socked Jon in the gut and then gave Peren a hard look.

Peren offered a sheepish smile. "Sorry."

"You got the better of me. Looks like the captain did right in picking you," he said, smiling back at her. "You're not bad on the eyes either."

"Yeah…you're not too bad, for a girl," Jon said with a wink.

"Where is Lukian?" asked Roi. "And what the hell were you doing in a tree? Does he know you were up there? He did find you, right?"

"He did," she confirmed. "He's up at the house."

Jon's brows met. "Why are you out here in a tree then? He's mighty overprotective of you, ma'am. I don't see him letting you go off into the night to climb trees for fun."

"Actually, I was supposed to stay in the house where he left me. He gave me strict instructions to remain there while he went to check out something that was bothering him."

"You listen well," added Roi with a snort.

"Thanks," said Peren, grinning. She was about to add more but stopped. A sinking feeling came over her. Something was wrong.

Lukian!

Her gaze snapped to Roi. "He's hurt."

"What?"

"He's hurt," she repeated.

"Who is?" asked Jon.

Peren touched her stomach lightly, the sinking feeling growing stronger with each passing second. "Lukian. He's hurt. I know it. I can feel it."

"Shit." Roi moved in closer to her. "You need to stay here with Jon. I'll go find the captain."

"I'm not staying out here. I'm going with you. He needs me."

Ignoring her outburst, Roi stared over her head at Jon. "Keep her out here and keep her safe."

"Will do," said Jon, talking as if she didn't get a say in the matter.

Roi looked faraway in thought for a moment and then touched her arm gently. "I've contacted the rest of the team. No one can reach Lukian. Lance and Wilson are close. Green is with Melanie and Missy. They're safe."

He hadn't called or radioed anyone, so she wasn't sure how he'd contacted the other men. She was about to ask when a red dot appeared on Jon's head.

"Get down!" yelled Roi, his body seeming to suddenly move in what felt like slow motion to her.

Peren threw her body toward Jon. In an instant, she was on him, knocking him to the ground. At the same second, it felt as if someone rammed a hot poker through her upper back.

Roi grabbed her and yanked her off Jon.

The next she knew he had dragged her into the woods and behind a large brick wall that had been erected to add privacy to the property.

Jon moved up next to her, his amber gaze wide. "You saved my life."

"Of course she did," Roi said matter-of-factly. He leaned over her and pulled Peren's shirt open. The cool night air on her breasts. She was more worried about the burning sensation that was growing in her chest than she was about her boobs showing.

She tried to reach up and see if, in fact, she was on fire. Roi caught her hands. He stared down at her with the same royal-blue eyes as Lukian and pushed her hair out of her face. He turned his head quickly toward the house and seemed to be listening to something that only he could hear.

"Lukian's made contact. He's in trouble," he said, his voice low. He glanced over at Jon. "Shift and go get the others. You'll make better time that way. Bring everything we've got in firepower and make sure Green comes with his medical supplies. Lukian is hurt, but he's not the one I'm most worried about now."

Peren knew without asking his concern was for her. "I'll be okay. I'm a fast healer… always have been," she said and coughed. Pain shot through her chest and she let out a small cry. "Wait? What do you mean by shift?

"Not the time to have this discussion," he said, putting pressure on her wound. "Whoever did this made sure to use a silver bullet. That's why you feel the burning. This strike has to be close to your heart. I don't know how you're talking and not dead. Green told us you don't just have werewolf blood in you, but all fucking kinds of supernatural DNA in you. Every shifter I know of has issues with silver and I'm pretty sure vamps do too. Now, as for the Fae and lower-level demon DNA in you, I'm not sure how that reacts to silver."

Peren lay there and soaked in Roi's words. *Vampires, Fae, shifters, demons?* Every fiber of her being wanted to protest, but she knew what he was saying was the truth. Hearing it said aloud was hard. She closed her eyes and took a minute to try to accept the information.

"You're a werewolf?" she asked awkwardly, unsure if she really wanted to hear him answer that.

"I can turn into a wolf, if that is what you mean. And before you ask, yes, I can lick my own balls when in shifted form." Roi bent his head closer to her. "Rest now. Jon will look after you. I'm going to go get Lukian and kill whoever fucking decided to play games with us tonight."

"My gut says you should wait for your team," said Peren.

Jon gulped. "After having nearly been killed, I'm going to say let's go with the little lady's gut." He yanked off his shirt and handed it to Peren.

She put it on and sat in stunned silence.

Chapter Thirty-Four

Lukian tried harder to reach Peren mentally. He failed. He did manage to reach his men telepathically, but it was a strain to do so. Roi was the only one he had an open link with. The bond between them had occurred because of the shared blood. The others he had to work at. He'd have a headache for a few days if he survived this, that much was sure—even if it wasn't for the bump on his head.

Roi opened his mind to him, but let him in only enough to acknowledge him, then pushed him away. He'd informed Lukian that he and Jon were with Peren, but that was all. His reluctance to notify him of Peren's status told Lukian that something was very wrong. He kept trying to reach Roi and Roi kept blocking him.

He yanked on the chains again. Someone had once told him of a lycanthrope that could regenerate severed limbs. He hoped this was true. He yanked harder and stopped only when he heard someone's low laugh.

"Yank all damn night, you fool. You can't get through them. Your lover is dead."

Dead? Peren was dead?

No, he would have felt the loss of her. Their bond was stronger now and would only continue to grow with time. He stopped moving and listened to the voice again. He couldn't get his body turned around to see who was talking, but the voice was familiar to him.

"It wasn't my intent to shoot her. I wanted only to fuck her and claim her as my mate. The bitch got in the way of me killing the sniper." A long sigh followed behind the man's statement. "I've carried the memory of the sweet taste of her blood with me for over ten years. I watched from a distance, waiting for her to be of an age that she could accept me and mate with me. The time has come."

Lukian's stomach tightened. This lunatic wanted to fuck his Peren, his lover, his wife. He had to fight the urge to vomit. And what did he mean, shoot her? Peren had been shot?

No!

"I wasn't sure she'd accept me. She'd turned down every man who'd ever asked her out and had never slept with a soul. As much as I wanted to be her first, I wanted more to know that she was my true mate. I bit the young one who caught her eye and watched as she took the man to her bed after that. His beast matured and he'd have been able to share his seed with her if I hadn't stepped in."

Lukian listened in disgust. This man—this thing—had purposely bitten another human to test compatibility? The man he'd done this to must have been Peren's fiancé, Kyle, the one she'd felt so guilty about when she was with him. The one who had gone missing.

"Did you kill him?" Lukian asked.

A sharp laugh answered his question. "Of course I killed him. He intended to make her his wife and impregnate her. I couldn't risk that. Every human I've fucked has left me unsatisfied since the transformation. I long to have my dick in the one meant for me."

It was Lukian's turn to laugh. "She's not meant for you, asshole! She's my mate now."

A boot hit him square between the shoulder blades. "You fool! Of course she's meant for you. I'm the reason it's so. If I hadn't bit her, she'd never have enough wolf blood in her to be your mate. I tasted bits of it in her when I attacked her, but the faerie was stronger. That's how she survived, you know... she unleashed her magic on me and sent me scurrying away like a mangy dog. I would have come back and finished her had I not recognized the potential for her to be my mate."

Lukian lifted his head and tried to turn to see the man. "How...why did you attack her to begin with?"

Another sharp laugh filled the room. "Because I wanted to wipe out Lakeland Matthews's loved ones and let him know what it was like to suffer before I killed him. It was his pipe dream that turned me into this. His dream and your blood, brother."

Lukian froze, understanding why the man's voice sounded so familiar. "Parker?"

Benjamin Parker was the man Roi had

replaced on the team. He'd been the one they'd assumed was dead all these years. Parker was right—he and Peren could be a match. Parker shared more of Lukian's DNA than Roi did, and the fact that Lukian and Peren were a mated pair meant that the potential for Peren and Parker to be a pair was extremely high, almost an absolute.

Parker let out a laugh. "Yes, it's me. Surprise, brother, I'm not dead."

"Dr. Matthews? Is he dead?" Lukian asked, concerned for Peren's father.

"Oh, I'm guessing he's combing the streets of New York City by now. I put a call in to him telling him that his daughter was being held overnight in a cell for disorderly conduct with those sluts she calls friends. And we all know how much he loves her. I mean, the man broke the rules and brought his work home with him, only for his first wife to inject herself with the same serums he helped to create—sure, he claims he didn't know she'd do it, but really, he had to see it coming. The crazy woman wanted a baby that bad. Bad enough to make herself a monster. I read all about it in his journals. Interesting reads."

Lukian let out his breath. Dr. Matthews was states away and safe. Peren was not. It didn't matter that Parker claimed she was dead, Lukian knew better. He didn't want to tip Parker off about Peren still being alive. The thought of him going after her again was too much for Lukian to bear. He fought to control his breathing and his body language. He didn't need to raise Parker's suspicions. Now, he just needed to buy his men time to get to him.

"So, what? Were you planning on killing Dr. Matthews and then convincing his daughter to fuck you and take you as her mate?" Saying the words was hard for him.

"No, I was planning on fucking his daughter first...making her my mate, then watching the look on her father's face when he saw who she would be forever tied to. I wanted so very much to have him know that she carried my child in her." He took a moment to laugh. "Ah, yes, 'the crazy one who couldn't stop the wolf from coming'... I'm sure the good doctor would have loved to know that I was fucking his daughter. He would have died wondering if she would turn out like her mother. But now—now—I'm afraid that I'll have to begin my search for a mate all over again. Seems like such a waste. She was quite the looker, too. Rare indeed in a mate."

Peren would never let this man near her. She'd sense the danger he presented and flee. At least that's what he hoped. He strained to draw in a breath. He had no doubt that Parker had broken at least two of his ribs. They'd heal within twenty minutes, but in the meantime, it hurt like hell every time he tried to move or talk.

Parker didn't give him a chance to voice his concerns. He leaned over him and whispered in his ear. "We met, you know... Peren and I. We dated. She liked me and was interested in me. We came close to having sex once, but it was too soon after the disappearance of the other for her to commit. I didn't want to raise her suspicions by pushing the issue with her. Hiring the Immortal Ops through various shell corporations and senators I bribed was just one more step in my end game. I wanted you to see me mate her. I wanted you to know she was supposed to be yours, but that in the end she ended up mine. And that was going to be the last thing you ever saw. But the bitch stepped in the path of my bullet."

Chapter Thirty-Five

"How the hell did she survive that?" Jon asked as he stood there staring at her in disbelief as Green bandaged her shoulder.

"Is this really necessary?" she asked melodiously.

The men surrounding her stopped suiting up in full combat gear and just looked at her. She watched as they all put matching headsets around the back of their heads and requested confirmation on being heard. These men were serious and she knew that they would die to save Lukian.

Jon seemed to be warming up to her. No surprise there. She had taken a bullet that would have been fatal for him. She glanced at the spot Green was bandaging. He'd managed to extract the bullet with almost no effort. He'd cleansed her wound and then waited. The burning stopped and was replaced by a cool, tingly feeling. Green monitored her body temperature and determined that she was healing her wounds internally first. He'd quickly explained how shifters heal themselves versus how vampires and Fae do it. He then had to explain what a Fae was to her. Turns out it was someone with magic. She had quite a bit to learn about supernaturals, but right now she was only worried about Lukian.

Lance pulled a black cap over his hair. She could see what had appealed to Melanie. He was a good-looking guy, but there was something about him that she couldn't put her finger on. He gave off a vibe that didn't make her feel entirely comfortable around him. She wondered if it was concern for Lukian, or his dislike for her.

Roi stepped forward. "Wilson and Lance are with me. We'll go in and eliminate any hostiles. Jon, you follow Green as soon as he gets Peren to the van. Secure the location. If you see anything moving that isn't us, shoot it."

"Be careful," she said, sitting up against Green's protests. "And bring Lukian back safe and unharmed."

Roi nodded. "We'll get him out. I

promise."

"I know," she answered softly.

Lance stepped forward. "Sir, with your permission, I'd like to swap out with Jon."

"Why?" asked Roi.

Wilson chambered a round in his weapon. "I don't give a shit who does what—can we get a move on this?"

Roi nodded. "Jon and Lance switch out."

*

Lukian lay in the darkened room and thought only of Peren as he tried to free himself from his chains. He needed to know if she was all right. His eyes drifted shut and he tried again to connect with Roi. This time Roi answered his call.

Brother, tell me of my mate.

Lukian felt that Roi's mood had improved, and Roi pushed tranquility out at him. *She is well. She is safe now, I promise you that.*

Lukian exhaled and let relief sweep over his body. It did not matter now if he survived, as long as Peren was okay.

Brother, should anything happen to me…

Nothing is going to happen to you so shut up.

Roi…there is another… Lukian was seized with a migraine so severe he felt the blood beginning to fall from his nose and the invisible cord that bonded them together crumbled. He would not be able to reach his men telepathically for a few more hours. He'd strained himself trying to find out about Peren and used up too much of his energy.

Chapter Thirty-Six

It had been over an hour since the men had taken off in search of Lukian. Peren sat quietly in the van and listened to the talk coming from Lance's headpiece. He'd turned it down in hopes that she wouldn't be able to pick up on it, but as nervous as she was she could have heard it a mile away. So far, a thorough search of the grounds had revealed nothing. They had concluded that Lukian must have been moved. Peren wasn't buying it. She still felt him here.

Lance leaned over and started the van. Peren felt her insides twist into a knot. She knew that Lukian was still here. She didn't know how or why, but she knew. She moved toward the door and put her hand on it.

"I know what you're thinking, and I wouldn't suggest doing it," Green said in his mild-mannered voice. "Roi will find the captain. Do not doubt his skills or loyalty to Lukian. They are, brothers after all, and that is a hard bond to break."

Peren smiled up at Green and tried to

appear weak and meager, but he wasn't buying it. She shrugged her shoulders and went with her gut instincts. She opened the door of the moving van and leapt out. The pavement came upon her fast and she rolled to avoid getting hurt.

*

Thaddeus Green watched the young one jump from the moving vehicle and had to hold back a smile. His instincts said to let her go. Allow her to do this. She would make a great queen to stand by Lukian's side with the wolves. When her mind was set on something, she went for it, no questions asked. Her composition was intriguing to him as well. He'd never encountered someone with DNA quite like hers and wanted to take a closer look at her. He wanted to help her unlock the keys to her strengths and powers. He wanted to monitor her every step of the way and document his findings.

Green also found himself liking Peren

because of her friends. Melanie in particular. He had unintentionally found himself reading Melanie's thoughts as they prepared to follow Jon back to aid Roi and Peren. She was still shaken by her experience with Lance. It had been strictly a sexual attraction between the two of them, or at least on her part. He knew Lance well enough to know that Melanie was the type of woman he'd fall for.

Melanie had helped Green pack up his supplies, surprising him with her knowledge of what he'd require in his bag, and then she'd given him a tiny hug before he left. He picked up on how attracted to him she was and how much she regretted not hooking up with him to begin with. She smelled of old Fae blood, and he wondered if in fact she possessed any magical skills that she was most likely unaware of. It was obvious she had received the faerie gift of seduction, but other than that he wasn't sure what she'd gotten.

Most humans had no idea if anything supernatural ran in their family. These were not matters that were discussed at dinner tables.

Green's mind wandered back to Melanie's long blonde locks. He wondered how it would feel to be running his hands through her hair while he fucked her. "Fucked" wasn't a word he used often, but it was what he wanted to do to her. He'd make love to her after that, but first he'd need to release himself. It had been decades since he'd had sex. The last woman he'd been with, he'd been in love with. She had died during childbirth—that's how they knew that a human could not carry a shifter's child to term. It had been a hard life lesson, one he did not care to repeat.

No matter how much he wanted a family, it would never be. He looked over at Lance as the van came to a stop. Lance was the closest thing he had to a brother. They shared the same strain of panther DNA.

"I've lost radio contact with the men," said Lance, a worried look on his face.

Green sighed. "I'll go shadow Peren, even though my gut says she'll be fine. You should find Roi and the others."

"Will do," said Lance, something off in his voice. "Green."

"Yes?"

"What do you think of Melanie?"

"Odd time for that question, isn't it?"

Lance met his gaze. "If something happened to me, you'd look out for her, right?"

Green wasn't sure what had prompted the question, but he nodded. "Of course I would."

"Good."

Chapter Thirty-Seven

Peren made her way quietly through the kitchen and in the direction of the east wing. The doorbell rang and made her jump. She soothed herself down when she thought about how absurd it would be for whoever had taken Lukian and shot her to bother with ringing the doorbell.

She peeked out the side window and was shocked to see Ben, one of the men Mel and Missy had fixed her up on a date with, standing there. She'd been horrible about returning his calls. What was he doing at her house? He had shit timing. Worried he'd get hurt in the commotion, she opened the door and smiled up at him.

"Umm...hi... I wasn't expecting to see you," she said. She didn't want to come out and say what bad timing he had.

Ben's lips curved into a thin smile and his crisp blue eyes glistened. Lukian's eyes were similar, but a much richer blue. In fact, Ben's hair was also similar to Lukian's. Thinking of

Lukian made her stomach tight. She needed to find him, but first she needed to get Ben out of harm's way.

"Peren, hi. Sorry to barge in on you like this, but I felt so bad for missing your birthday that I had to stop by the minute my schedule allowed."

He was a nice guy and she felt bad for having to be so short with him, but now really wasn't the time. "Now's not really a good time, Ben. Do you think it'd be all right for me to call you later in the week?"

His blue gaze settled upon her and her body warmed. He took a step in toward her and forced her to back away from the door. "Peren, I drove over an hour from the airport just to see you. I'm not asking for much of your time. A quick drink and permission to use your restroom would be much appreciated."

"Of course, I'm sorry, I forgot my manners."

She backed up and allowed him to enter. The faintest hint of musk moved past her nose as he walked by and her legs tightened. Her body reacted to his presence, but her mind and heart were focused solely on Lukian. Ben turned to her and smiled, innocent at first, then sexy.

His black turtleneck and black dress slacks made him look like he was ready to head out on the town. Peren looked down and noticed the mud caked to his boots. Boots? What an odd pairing with dress pants. Ben noticed her staring down at his boots and coughed.

"Sorry for the mud. I parked my car down at the end of the drive. The gate was open slightly, but not enough for my car to fit through, so I had to walk up. I must have stepped in a few mud puddles on the way."

Peren noticed a speck of dried reddish brown on Ben's hand. She didn't need him to confirm what it was, she could smell it—it was blood. Everything began to line up: his appearance out of nowhere, his bad timing, his awkward behavior, the blood.

Her gut screamed at her to run, to get away from him. She resisted and stayed perfectly still. "I'm sorry, Ben, but I don't remember having ever given you this address. I know I gave you my apartment one, but…oh well…it must have slipped my mind."

Ben smiled and took a step toward her. "No, no you didn't give me this address. I called your friend's house and she was kind enough to point me in the right direction."

Red flags shot up in Peren's head. Melanie and Missy were both still at the safe house. There was no way he'd gotten a hold of one of them. He was lying. Her body became rigid and Ben's facial expression changed. She did her best to calm down but failed miserably at it. She closed her eyes for a moment to collect her thoughts and felt faint.

Peren! She heard Lukian's voice in her head.

She almost answered him aloud but managed to catch herself before she did. *Are you okay? Where are you? What happened?*

I'm fine. I think that I'm still on the manor grounds. I'm not sure…I'm in a cell of some sort.

"Peren, are you all right? Do you need to lie down?" Ben asked.

Her eyes snapped open. Ben was next to her, holding her elbow. She jerked her arm away and then stopped in midmotion. She put her hand to her head to indicate that she had a headache and then peeked out at him.

"I think I'm coming down with a migraine. I should probably call it a night. Thank you for the birthday wishes and for stopping by."

Ben moved closer to her. His leg brushed against her thigh and she knew that he was hard and ready for her. Suddenly, her nose filled with the scent of want, desire, sex, some her own, but mostly his. He wanted to fuck her right here and now.

Peren, what's going on? Who's there with you? Is that Roi? Lukian's voice was full of concern for her.

She tried to block the thoughts of Ben that came to her, but she was too late. Lukian saw him too. *Get away from him! Go! He's the one who killed your stepmother…he's the wolf that attacked you in the woods when you were little!*

Ben touched her arm again, and she felt her body react with a jolt of power. A tingling sensation began in her midsection, much like the orgasms Lukian was so good at causing and radiated up and out her arms. She wasn't sure what to do with all this *new* energy until Lukian came to her mind. She knew then that she could help him or die trying. She thrust the power out and willed it in Lukian's direction.

Ben came at her with elongated fingers. His teeth lengthened and his voice seemed raspier. He looked demonic, half-man, half-beast. "I've waited too long for this. I won't wait anymore."

"Ben?"

He sneered and then sniffed the air, his gaze narrowing in on her. "You let him claim you. Mate you."

"Who?" she asked, hoping to buy time.

"Lukian," he said, snarling. "I don't care that you're his wife now. I saw you first. You're going to be mine. You'll birth my children, not his."

Lukian's wife?

Lukian was suddenly in her head again. *I'm coming. Hold on.*

She blinked at Ben, her thoughts held firmly to Lukian. *I'm your wife? Is that what being a mate means?*

Yes. You are. Get used to it. It's unbreakable.

Ben reached for her and the idea of letting him touch her sickened her. Peren ducked down and ran under his arm. She caught him by surprise and made it through unharmed. She ran full-force toward the front door. The weight of Ben's body slammed into her, sending her flying to the ground. She screamed as she slammed the back of her head into his face. Doing this afforded her much-needed time to push him off her. She rolled to her feet and ran for the door. It opened before she got to it and she found herself face-to-face with Lance and Green. She'd built up too much momentum and was unable to stop herself from slamming into Green. She sent him hurtling back out the door and his gun flying to the floor, before landing square on her backside.

Something moved behind her and she knew that she had just afforded Ben the opportunity to arm himself. Something burst past her. She caught only a glimpse of it but it didn't look human. Nor did it sound human. It sounded like a giant beast.

There was the sudden sound of gunfire all around her and she waited, expecting to be hit again, but no pain came. Someone grabbed her, shielding her with their body, and they both fell to the ground with a hard thud.

As quickly as the hail of bullets had started, it stopped, and for a bit, she heard nothing beyond ringing in her ears. It took her a moment to realize what was happening as someone ripped her up and off the ground, and the heavy weight that had been on her was no more. She blinked to find Lukian there, checking her, touching her all over, concern dancing across his handsome face.

Roi was suddenly there too, yanking on Lukian, yelling. It took a bit for the ringing to stop before Peren could make out what was being said. "It's not her blood, Captain!"

Not my blood?

Looking down, Peren found that she was

covered in blood. It soaked her clothing, her hair, everything. Had she been shot again? Was her wound bleeding? She touched the spot she'd been struck earlier, only to find the skin was healed over completely, as if it had never happened.

Roi continued to yank on Lukian, and Wilson came to his assistance. Peren turned slowly and found Jon bent over, near Green—who was working frantically on someone. But who? Peren took a small step forward and the patient came into view.

Lance.

His lifeless body was on the ground, where Peren had been. The realization that Lance had protected her from Ben's gunfire at great cost to himself hit Peren hard. She fell forward, shaking her head, knowing deep down that Lance's injuries weren't ones that would heal. From the expression on the men's faces, they knew it too.

Peren reached for Lukian, and he stopped struggling with Roi and seemed to calm almost instantly. He grabbed for her hand and Roi let him past. Lukian bent and then went to his knees in front of her. He drew her into his powerful arms.

"It's over," he whispered. "You're safe and it's over."

"But Lance," she protested.

"I know, baby," he replied. "I know."

The tears broke free as she hugged her husband tight.

Chapter Thirty-Eight

Peren touched Lukian's arm gently. Fog covered the cemetery grounds and the cool morning air set a chill in her bones. She glanced over the group of men—the I-Ops, as Lukian had later explained to her.

Green and Wilson stood across the casket from them, while Roi stood tall on the other side of Lukian. She knew this was hard for them. One of their team had fallen in the line of duty. Lance had died protecting her. He'd taken bullets meant for her while Lukian had charged past them in partially shifted form and had ripped Ben to pieces—but not before Ben had unloaded multiple rounds into Lance.

The Ops stood strong as a unit around the casket. Their expressions were unreadable, as if they'd seen too much death in their years to let it show now. She knew they were hurting.

Guilt for being the reason Lance was dead weighed heavily on her. Lukian had told her more than once in the past week that it wasn't her fault. She knew better. Lance died protecting her.

Melanie and Missy were in attendance to pay their respects—though they had not been told all the details. As far as they knew, a kidnapping attempt on Peren had gone bad, the men had saved her, and Lance had died. No one had told them the truth of the Immortal Ops team, or that supernaturals were real. That men who could shift into animals weren't the stuff of myths and legends. And that Peren had fallen totally and completely in love with one—and was now considered his wife.

That had been Peren's decision. She'd hoped that by keeping that part of the story from them, she'd somehow protect them. The casket in front of her told her just how dangerous the world of supernaturals was. She didn't want to stand over Melanie's or Missy's grave.

Lukian's muscles tightened and she knew that he was fighting to remain in control of his emotions. She stood on her tiptoes and kissed his cheek. He bent down and turned his face to meet her lips.

I love you so much. His voice rang out in her head. She felt the warmth of his lips on hers as he kissed her tenderly.

I love you too.

The End

Dear Reader

Did you enjoy this title and want to know more about Mandy M. Roth, her pen names, and all the titles she has available for purchase (over 100)?

About Mandy:

New York Times & *USA TODAY* Bestselling Author Mandy M. Roth is a self-proclaimed Goonie, loves 80s music and movies, and wishes leg warmers would come back into fashion. She also thinks the movie *The Breakfast Club* should be mandatory viewing for...okay, everyone. When she's not dancing around her office to the sounds of the 80s or writing books, she can be found designing book covers for New York publishers, small presses, and indie authors.

Learn More:

To learn more about Mandy and her pen names, please visit http://www.mandyroth.com

For latest news about Mandy's newest releases

and sales, subscribe to her newsletter:
http://www.mandyroth.com/newsletter/
To join Mandy's Facebook Reader Group: The Roth Heads, please visit
https://www.facebook.com/groups/MandyRothReaders/

Review this title:

Please let others know if you enjoyed this title. Consider leaving an honest review on the vendor site from which you purchased this title. Reviews help to spread the word and boost overall sales. This means more books in the series you love.

Thank you!